Praise

"*Gravesend* is one of these novels that connects so deeply, it'll make you wonder why you spent so much time and energy on all these other novels who fail to connect the dots and expose the visceral truths of crime. When a novel is this good, you get kind of feverish about it." –Benoît Lelièvre, *Dead End Follies*

"Like Thomas Hardy and Bernard Malamud before him, Boyle is many things at once. He is a novelist who, as Auden said a novelist must, knows how to be just among the just and filthy among the filthy. He is a wordsmith with all the devices of nineteenth- and twentieth-century novels at his disposal. He is, in short, a damn good storyteller." –Alex Shakespeare, *North Dakota Quarterly*

"William Boyle's *Gravesend* is a pitch-perfect depiction of the titular Brooklyn neighborhood, one where Italian, Irish, and Russian-Americans still hold sway, and where hipsterism and hip-hop are foreign ideals that infect the wayward children of a dying generation. It's almost a cliché that authors live in Brooklyn now, but few of the current crop have written about that overpriced borough in the way native son Boyle does." –Nick Mamatas, *The Big Click*

"Boyle's writing is raw, poetic, unflinching, nostalgic and perverse. Urgency inhabits his pages, and the characters live on weeks after you put the book down. *Gravesend* is a novel read in a day, and then read again, slowly." –Anya Groner, *L.A. Review of Books*

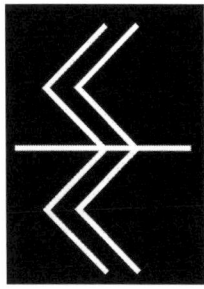

A Broken River Books collection

Broken River Books
10765 SW Murdock Lane
Apt. G6
Tigard, OR 97224

Copyright © 2015 by William Boyle

Cover art and design copyright © 2015 by Matthew Revert
www.matthewrevert.com

Interior design by J David Osborne

All rights reserved. No part of this book may be reproduced or transmitted in any form or by any means, electronic or mechanical, including photocopying, recording, or by any information storage and retrieval system, without the written consent of the publisher, except where permitted by law.

This is a work of fiction. All names, characters, places, and incidents are the product of the author's imagination. Where the names of actual celebrities or corporate entities appear, they are used for fictional purposes and do not constitute assertions of fact. Any resemblance to real events or persons, living or dead, is coincidental.

ISBN: 978-1-940885-19-3

Printed in the USA.

DEATH DON'T HAVE NO MERCY

stories

WILLIAM BOYLE

BROKEN RIVER BOOKS
PORTLAND, OR

*In memory of
my grandfather and Uncle Joe*

TABLE OF CONTENTS

Death Don't Have No Mercy

1

Yank Byrd's Idea for a Book,
Late Summer 1992

17

Poor Box

29

Zero at the Bone

51

Far from God

69

Poughkeepsie

91

In the Neighborhood

113

Here Come the Bells

141

"Death don't have no mercy in this land."
　　　　　　　　–Reverend Gary Davis

DEATH DON'T HAVE NO MERCY

Calhoun wasn't quite sure why he'd stolen the Walkman from the kid. Maybe just out of curiosity. It wasn't like Calhoun stole things often. He could count on one hand everything he had ever lifted. When he was in grammar school at Our Lady of the Sorrows, he'd snagged a quarter from the offertory basket during Mass. When he was a freshman in college, he'd stolen a pair of his girlfriend's sister's panties while he was at their house for Thanksgiving. He hadn't sniffed them or done anything weird with them, but it had calmed him down pressing them between his fingers. Most recently, Calhoun had stolen a twenty off the bar at The Fort from his Uncle John's bill pile. And that was all. Now there was the Walkman.

The thing that had really attracted Calhoun to the Walkman was the fact that it was just a plain cassette deck, the type he'd once owned. It was rare to see a kid these days with one of those. Mostly they carried sleek little iPods or portable CD players. But this kid, a little black kid dressed in worn jeans and a green sweatshirt, had this old Walkman. Calhoun wanted to know what he was listening to. Maybe that was the reason he'd stolen it.

It wasn't hard to steal the Walkman. Calhoun walked about a hundred paces behind the kid for a mile or so. Finally, he met up with some of his buddies at the basketball courts over by St. Raymond's Cemetery on East Tremont and put the Walkman down on a bench, tying the earplugs around the deck. Calhoun just looked like some half-respectable middle-aged guy out for a walk, stopping to watch a group of kids play ball. No one saw Calhoun lean down over the bench and scoop up the Walkman. He walked away from the courts quickly. When he was at a safe distance, he put in the earplugs and listened. This kid was special. The tape, which he had rewound to the beginning of Side A, started with Memphis Minnie's "Killer Diller Blues." After that was Hank Williams's "Lost Highway" and Blind Willie McTell's "East St. Louis Blues." Calhoun was floored. He walked around until it was dark and finished listening to the tape. There were songs by Fats Domino, Reverend Gary Davis, Sister Rosetta Tharpe, The Carter Family, Johnny Cash, Robert Johnson, and John Lee Hooker. When he got home, he put the tape into the cassette deck on his stereo and listened to it again as he prepared a light dinner of salad and scrambled eggs.

The next day Calhoun walked all around looking for the kid, but there was no sign of him. He had dubbed a copy of the tape and was hoping to somehow return the Walkman without revealing himself as the thief. But he didn't find the kid. Calhoun met his Uncle John and they had dinner together and split three pitchers of Coors Light. Calhoun stumbled home at about nine-thirty, listening to the songs and singing along. He had known all of the songs by heart long before hearing them on the kid's tape, but they had become new to him somehow.

Calhoun woke up the following morning with a bad hangover. His mother called. "Kevin," she said. "It's Saturday."

"I know," he said.

"You promised you'd give me a ride to Aunt Lucy's."

"Shit."

"Uncle John said you were out late with him last night."

"Not late."

"You're wasting your life away. Living in that dark little apartment. Drinking. I don't know why you quit that teaching job."

"Ma, not now."

"Can you give me a ride?"

"I'll be over in ten minutes."

"We can take Uncle John's car. It's parked on Revere."

Calhoun got dressed, brushed his teeth, and walked over to his mother's house on Harding. It was true what she had said. He never should have quit his job teaching at Preston. He had been a history teacher and now he was a bum. He wasn't sure why he had quit. For the same reason, he guessed, that he had stolen the kid's Walkman. Curiosity. If it wasn't for his buddy Ralph letting him live on the arm in his basement apartment, he'd really be done for.

Calhoun's mother was waiting on the front stoop when he got to her house. "Now I'll be an hour late," she said.

"I'm sorry."

His mother handed him the keys to Uncle John's Oldsmobile. "Uncle John gave me these on Wednesday. He hasn't driven the car in a week. He says he hopes it starts."

"It'll start. Weather's been nice enough."

They walked over to Revere and found the car. Calhoun opened the passenger door for his mother and helped her in. He opened the driver's side door and got in under the wheel. He started the car and let it run for a minute. As he waited, he took the kid's tape out of his jacket pocket and pressed it into the tape deck. "Killer Diller Blues" kicked in.

His mother smiled. "I like this," she said.

Calhoun wasn't expecting that. He had figured she would tell him to turn it down, the way she always did when they drove together. One time he had put in *Music from Big Pink* and she had turned red, demanding that he turn it down and telling him that it was junk. Now, surprised, he said nothing. His mother moved her head to the music.

They drove over the Throgs Neck Bridge and got to Aunt Lucy's in Gravesend before Side A was finished on the kid's tape. No traffic. Not even around JFK. Calhoun helped his mother out of the car. "Why don't you come in?" she said.

"No thanks," Calhoun said.

His mother showed no sign of disappointment. "Pick me up at six," she said, and then she walked up to Aunt Lucy's front door and knocked.

Calhoun waited until she was safely inside and then drove off. He knew a bar on Avenue U called Joe V's Lounge. His old girlfriend Tonya, who was from Coney Island, had taken him there a few times. He wondered if he would run into her. He hoped he would. He could use an old girlfriend right about now. Especially one like Tonya.

He got a spot in front of the bar, which was even more of a dive than he remembered, and waited until "Me and the Devil Blues" was done and then he shut down the car and went inside. The bartender was a miserable codger who wore his thinning white hair slicked back, his nose hanging in the middle of his face like a deformed squash. A puffy blonde in the corner sucked on a bottle of MGD and a kid with a no chin and a prosthetic leg swept the floor. It was a real hellish scene.

Calhoun bellied up to the bar and ordered a bottle of Coors Light. He fanned out three bucks. The codger popped the top off a bottle and brought it over, scooping the money off the bar. Calhoun drank.

Soon enough the puffy blonde came over. She wasn't his ex-girlfriend, but she was the owner of a warm box and a warm box was all he needed. She had an extra layer of meat on her that colored in her curves, and the cheap black dress she wore showed off the rounded tops of her breasts. Her hair was platinum, and she smelled like she had just blasted herself with some fruity body spray. Whatever she'd done, she couldn't cover the stink of whiskey on her breath or the hot odor blooming from her armpits.

Calhoun had a few hours to kill.

"Buy me a beer?" she said.

"Why not?" Calhoun said.

The bartender brought one over and Calhoun paid for it.

The blonde went straight to work. After a few championship pulls off the bottle, she said, "I'm Shelley."

"I'm Kevin."

"You got a cigarette?"

He shook his head.

She leaned over the bar and those breasts went with her, flopping forward and pressing down on a couple of damp-looking coasters. "You got a cigarette, Crutch?" she asked the codger.

Crutch came over and gave her a Pall Mall, lighting it with a wooden match scraped against the underside of the bar. As she sucked on her cigarette, she began talking. She held her cigarette in one hand, letting the ash grow long before tipping it into an ashtray, and with her other hand she tapped her long red nails on the bar top. Her nails were only grown out and polished on that one hand. On her cigarette hand, the nails were bitten low and unpainted. She was telling Calhoun where she was from, where she had gone to school, about her old job at Meat Supreme.

Calhoun sat there and tried to imagine what Shelley's breasts looked like sprung from the tight wrap of that cheap dress.

Shelley took a long drag on her cigarette and

continued talking.

Calhoun had no idea what she was going on about, but it didn't matter. She put out her cigarette and they finished their beers at the same time. "What next?" Calhoun said.

"My place," she said. "It's a five minute drive. You got a car?"

Fifteen minutes later, Calhoun and Shelley were driving down Avenue U. Calhoun had the kid's tape going at full volume. Shelley didn't seem to like it. She shouted directions over the blare of "Lost Highway" and "I'm Bad Like Jesse James."

When they got to her place, a walk-in on Bay Thirty-Fourth, Calhoun insisted on staying in the car to hear the end of Johnny Cash's "Flesh and Blood." It was the last song on the kid's tape. He expected Shelley to say that it was a pretty song, but she didn't. Calhoun thought about walking out on the whole show. He wasn't thinking straight anyway. He was just looking for a piece. If Shelley could at least appreciate these songs, maybe then he'd go inside with her. But it had been a couple of weeks since he had slept with a woman and Calhoun was hungry for it. Didn't matter what music she liked.

They went inside. It was a modest apartment, somewhere between a shithole and the kind of apartment that grandmothers usually died in. No pictures on the wall. She had a clock radio out on the counter top in the kitchen, an automatic coffeepot, and not much else. In the bedroom, several pairs of black nylons and brassieres were strewn on the floor like bunched-up parachutes. Shelley immediately went to the bathroom to take a shower. Calhoun sat on the edge of bed.

After about fifteen minutes, Shelley came out of the bathroom. Her blonde hair was combed straight back and she was wearing a towel. "Here I am, Kevin," she said.

"There you are," Calhoun said.

She dropped the towel. Those breasts didn't look so bad hanging loose. She approached him, sat down on his lap, and began to kiss his face and neck. "I'm lucky you walked into that place today," she said.

Calhoun took his shirt off. "We're both lucky."

She helped him out of his pants and boxers. He watched her. "I'm sorry I'm fat," she said. "I've always been fat."

"Doesn't matter."

"You think I'm ugly?"

"You're pretty."

"Pretty fat. I'm good in bed, though."

When they were done, they sat in silence on the bed and shared a cigarette. Calhoun rarely smoked, but he was out of breath and he needed one. Shelley hadn't been kidding. She was good. Calhoun got up and went into the kitchen to see what time it was. The red digits on the clock radio flashed 5:35. He got dressed. Shelley tugged at his pants, trying to convince him to stay. She gave a hangdog face.

"I've got to pick up my mother at six," Calhoun

said. "She'll be angry if I make her wait."

"Can't you take her home and come back?"

"No, I'm in The Bronx."

"Can I come visit you in The Bronx some time?"

"Sure."

"Give me your number."

He wrote it for her on the pad that she handed him.

"I'll call you," she said. "Maybe we can do something tomorrow night."

"Sure, Shelley."

Calhoun picked his mother up at Aunt Lucy's and they drove home together in silence, listening to the kid's tape on low. His mother knew that he had no interest in hearing about the party, so she said nothing. He didn't feel like talking. He was thinking about Shelley. He was looking forward to seeing her.

He dropped his mother off at her house and helped her inside. She asked if he wanted tea. He said no. She thanked him for the ride, reluctantly gave him twenty bucks the way she always did, and he left. He brought the Oldsmobile back to Uncle John's house on Mayflower and parked it in the driveway. He ejected the kid's tape from the deck and put it in his breast pocket. Later, he would listen to it on the Walkman. He went up to his Uncle John's front door and knocked, but there was no answer. He left the keys in the mailbox. From Mayflower, he walked back to East Tremont. In no time at all, he was sitting at the bar in The Fort with a pint of Guinness and a shot of Jameson in front of him. Red Irene was bartending. She was from Galway, and she had a rear end to stop a snowplow.

Red Irene said, "Kevin, where's your uncle?"

"Haven't seen him today," Calhoun said. "I stopped by his house, but he wasn't home."

"I've got something for him. If you run into him, tell him to come see me here tonight. Or tomorrow night. Next round's on me."

Calhoun drank in the neighborhood on the spoils of his Uncle John's generosity. He couldn't go into a bar—The Fort or Casey's or Paddy Doherty's—without having a drink lined up for him. It certainly wasn't his generosity that the bartenders and other bar patrons were rewarding. He rarely had more than twenty or thirty bucks on him. His Uncle John was a god in the neighborhood, the kind of upper-class barfly that every true drinker aspired to be.

Red Irene was back in front of Calhoun, pouring a Bloody Mary for Ben Bethlehem, who was sitting down at the end of the bar reading the *Post*. "Got a glow about you tonight," she said. "You in love?"

"Freshly laid," Calhoun said.

Red Irene flashed her sharp yellow teeth. "I know her?"

"Nope."

"Come on."

"You don't."

"Renee from the bank?"

"Out of my league, Red. Like you. I'm a lifer in the minors."

"What's her name?"

"Fat Shelley."

"Fat Shelley?"

"Fat Shelley from Gravesend." Calhoun was the one smiling now.

"Sounds like a winner." Red Irene turned and humped down to the end of the bar, putting the Bloody Mary in front of Ben. Ben didn't look up from his paper.

Calhoun finished his Guinness and chased it with the Jameson. Then he took Red Irene up on that free round. After that, Ben Bethlehem bought him one. Then Dennis Moran, who had come in with his wife and kid for the Steak & Shrimp dinner special that was such a big draw. Within the hour, Calhoun was loaded. Red Irene called a cab for him. He took the ride and used what was left of the twenty his mother had given him to pay the driver.

When he got home, he found the Walkman, inserted the kid's tape in the deck, and listened from start to finish. He wondered if the kid had made the tape or if someone had made it for him. The transitions were excellent. Calhoun had always paid close attention to the transitions between songs in mixtapes. Back when he would make mixes for old girlfriends, he considered himself a champ at transitions. Sometimes he still thought of one stretch of songs on a mixtape that he had made for Tonya, the girl from Coney. The way the songs tumbled into each other. It was something worth cheering. Worth remembering. What he was remembering now was the way four songs ended side B of the tape he'd made for Tonya two weeks before they had split. Elvis's "Kentucky Rain" had bled perfectly into "Poison Love" by Johnnie & Jack. Then there was "Buried Bones" by Tindersticks and, finally, "Who Are

You This Time" by Tom Waits. Calhoun felt that the way he'd aligned those songs had really been saying something to Tonya. He had put a lot of effort into the tape, especially that last sequence of songs, so it hurt pretty hard when Tonya crushed the tape underfoot outside Nathan's in some kind of fit.

The kid had those kinds of transitions there on his tape. The kind that haunted you. "I'm Bad Like Jesse James" leading into "Trouble in Mind." Calhoun thought that he might cook up a mixtape for Shelley. Show off his abilities. His record and cassette collection had dwindled because he'd sold most of what he owned for booze money, but there were still a few old records and cassettes around. He had that Hank album that he'd never sell, Cash's Folsom Prison and San Quentin albums, a few Leadbelly records, two by Skip James, *Otis Blue* by Otis Redding, three or four blues compilations, and cassettes of *Rain Dogs* and *Frank's Wild Years* by Tom Waits. It wasn't as much as he used to have, but it got him through. Yeah, he'd make a tape for Shelley tomorrow, he decided. No matter if she didn't dig the music he was into.

In the morning, he got to work. It was the best cure for his hangover. He sat at the kitchen table, drinking water from a pint glass, eating a toasted bagel, and figuring out a possible song list. He crossed off songs he thought Shelley would find too depressing in favor of more upbeat tunes.

Around noon, he got dressed. He walked to the dollar store on East Tremont and bought a blank cassette tape. He went back home and began dubbing songs, trying to match ends with beginnings and doing the math to make sure he came in just a few seconds under sixty minutes.

By the time he finished, it was dark and he was hungry. He kept expecting Shelley to call, but she never did. He thought about calling his Uncle John and asking to borrow the Olds again, but he didn't want to seem desperate. He'd feel like a heel if he showed up at Joe V's begging after Shelley. He decided to wait for another hour. If she didn't call by then, he figured, he'd go to The Fort.

Shelley never called. Calhoun put the finished mixtape in his jacket pocket and went to The Fort. His Uncle John was there, and the drinks started coming. First there was the pitcher of Coors Light. Then there were a few shots of Jameson. Dave Keelan came in and bought Calhoun a pint of Guinness. Red Irene was bartending. She wore tight black cargo pants that made him forget all about Fat Shelley. The night wasn't so bad after all.

Calhoun stayed at the bar until closing time. He hit on Red Irene and helped her clean up. She laughed at him. "Give me a chance," he said. "You're the Yankees. The Cardinals. And I'm the Pawtucket Shitheels. All washed up."

"You're cute," Red Irene said and that gave him hope.

"Cute is shit."

"What happened to Fat Shelley?"

"I'm over her. She probably ate too much and fell

asleep in the gutter. Come on, Red. Let's spend the night together. I won't tell anyone. Tomorrow we can forget it."

"I've got to close up."

Calhoun took the tape he had made for Shelley out of his jacket pocket and put it on the bar.

"What's that?" Red Irene said.

"A mixtape," Calhoun said. "I made it for you."

"A mixtape? How 1992 of you." Red Irene took the tape and looked at the track list. "Looks good."

"I'm good at making them. Listen for the transitions."

"Thank you." Red put the tape in the pocket on her right thigh.

"You wanna slum it in the minors for a night, you let me know."

Red laughed.

Calhoun left the bar and decided to head to the park where he'd stolen the kid's Walkman. When he got there, he sat down on the bench he'd lifted the deck from and looked around. The park was empty. Calhoun didn't know what to do. He felt lost. He thought about Red Irene in those tight black cargo pants. He thought about Shelley's apartment, bare, just the clock radio and coffeepot. He thought about the kid's tape, the top-shelf transitions, the surprising mix of blues and classic country.

He heard some footsteps behind him and turned. It was Ben Bethlehem, wasted to high holy hell. He was wearing a big bomber jacket that hung loose on him.

"Ben?" Calhoun said.

Ben sat down next to him.

"What are you doing over here?"

"I'm just here."

They sat there in silence for a while. Calhoun got up and left, walking away up East Tremont. Ben followed him. Calhoun turned and said, "You following me?"

"No," Ben said.

"You sure?"

It was then that Calhoun saw something dark pass over Ben Bethlehem's eyes. A grim crookedness that he could just make out in the low light of early morning. Ben bared his teeth. Calhoun thought about turning tail and booking it. He wondered if Ben had gone off the deep end. There had always been something sinister about him, about the way he ordered Bloody Marys from Red Irene, about the way he read the *Post* down at the darkened corner of the bar.

Calhoun didn't run. He just stood there. The knife was out in Ben's hand before he knew what was happening. Ben snapped it at him. It went in above his ribs. Calhoun felt pain that was hot and sharp. He choked on his breath.

Ben, slurring his words, said, "I followed you. I followed you the other day too. When you stole that kid's radio. I followed you to Brooklyn. I followed you before that. I followed you when you taught at Preston."

Calhoun went down, bleeding out on the sidewalk. He said, "What did I do?"

"Nothing," Ben said, and the word rang in Calhoun's ears. *Nothing*. It was shitty word when it was used the wrong way. The worst word of them all.

Ben leaned over and pulled the knife out. Calhoun put his hand over the wound and felt the blood pouring out through his fingers. He didn't care if he died, and he didn't care if he had no idea at all why Ben Bethlehem had stabbed him. At that moment, his only hope was that the kid whose Walkman he'd stolen would find him in a few hours and call the police. That kid was special, he knew it. He could sense it. Calhoun wanted the kid to remember him for something. For some reason. Even if only as the dead man he found on East Tremont near the park where he'd lost his Walkman. After all, that was the kind of thing that stayed with a kid. That shaped a life.

YANK BYRD'S IDEA FOR A BOOK, LATE SUMMER 1992

Yank Byrd addressed the letter to the editors of *Broken Spoke* and then typed:

I hope like hell you'll consider the enclosed story, "The Incredible Bright Life of the Snatch Pie Coeds." I have previously published stories in CRABS FOR YOUR MOTHER, THE ETERNAL GLORY, and TEAR DOWN THE WALL. I am from The Bronx. Thanks for your time.

He rolled the paper out of the Royal and stuffed it in the envelope with the ten page stunner of a story. It was the best work he'd done. The part where one of the coeds shot a ping pong ball out of her puss and nailed Rivera the Maintenance Man in the eye—that was golden goddamn stuff.

Yank sealed and stamped the envelope and went down to the post office on East Tremont. Nancy was working and she always brightened up his day, saying things like, "God bless you, Yank" and then clicking her long red nails on the other side of the glass and asking if his package was liquid or perishable even though she knew it was just a whopper of a story.

After the post office, Yank went to MacDougal's for an Irish whiskey, God's own rocket boost to the day. The old men looked at their racing forms as Yank watched the scores on the big-screen TV over the bar. The Yanks had dropped another one to the Twins. Their pitchers were shitting the bed. Yank had his name because as a kid he always wore a number seven Mickey Mantle jersey and a battered old Yankee cap around the neighborhood. It got so that he sometimes forgot his real name was Murphy. The first story he had ever written—when he was seven and Mantle was in his fourteenth glorious season—had been a story about the Mick whipping the balls off an oil baron behind an old abandoned gas station. It had never really happened—he had never heard of such a thing—but it was then that he saw the limitless power of stories.

Doc came over and said, "Yank, how's a boy?"

"Aces, Doc. All the way."

"And your mother?"

"Gonna live to be two hundred. All that vermouth."

"Another?"

"Sure, thanks."

Doc poured, and Yank threw it back in one graceful motion. The whiskey burned and went down only as it could in the morning.

Doc walked away, slinging a bleach-soaked dishrag over his shoulder, and then he came back over, poised to pour another. "You hear anything from your fuckstain brother?"

Yank nodded. "Hands Down is out."

"Liked it better when they called him Jimmy the Shit."

"Cousin Eugene called. Said Hands Down is moving to Michigan."

"Michigan? Bullshit. He'll come begging after your mother. Come back and give you hell. The way he used to. He shows up, you put him straight. He don't own you. Can't tell you what to do."

"He's not coming back."

"I sure as shit hope not."

Yank tapped the bar and left. The whiskeys from Doc were always on the house. Doc loved Yank's mother like a sister. They had grown up together in adjoining houses that got torn down when the Cross Bronx Expressway went in. Doc liked to talk about how the neighborhood had a lot of pig farms back then. He looked back on those days with fondness and Yank was glad for it since he didn't have the cash to spare for morning whiskey. The magazines he'd listed in his letter to *Broken Spoke* weren't real. No one had ever accepted one of his stories. He had submitted to all of the big guns and they had all sent back form rejections. He had started submitting stories to magazines with crazy names that operated out of places like Blue Fuck Falls, Oregon and Panda Puss, Tennessee. They still came back rejected. Two hundred stories maybe, and he kept them in the open top of a broken player piano in the basement of his mother's house. They were wrapped in twine, many of them yellowed at the edges, and they were the kind of stories that someday someone would find and go off fucking themselves in the ear for not having caught on sooner.

When Yank got home he went back to work on the Royal. A new story was cooking about a homeless guy who skateboarded around Hunts Point on a board made out of a piece of the True Cross. He thought it was time for a religious sort of story. He poured a coffee and started to peck at the typewriter.

He got the first sentence down and stopped. He looked up at the wall where he kept a picture of Mantle knocking one into the heaven-high right-field seats, twisting his body, caught in an *oomph*, blood probably bubbling at his waist like some sweet tough angel sent to redeem the world. The picture always got him going.

He typed the next sentence and it was the kind of beauty that made him want to cream himself right then and there. He wasn't sure where some of the stuff came from. It was just in the air and he caught it was the way he liked to think about it. But that didn't account for the talent. Not one bit. This guy on the skateboard, he was priceless. Pure Yank.

Yank's mother had false teeth, eyes that drooped, and scaly skin. She wore thin housedresses that dwelled over her bony frame. Yank sometimes thought it was a scarecrow sneaking up on him, offering a sandwich and a bowl of nuts. Yank was pecking away when he turned to see her poking a plate at his face. "A sandwich," she said. "And almonds. You gotta eat."

Yank crossed his arm over the typewriter carriage. "I told you not to sneak up on me."

"I'm not looking. You never let me read your stories. How come?"

"Ma."

"Eat the sandwich."

Yank took the sandwich and a handful of nuts. He put an almond between his teeth.

"Cousin Eugene called again," his mother said. "He's bringing your brother home."

Yank spit up some almond gristle.

"Just for a day or two."

"Hands Down's coming home?"

"Don't worry, honey." His mother reached out and rubbed his nose the way she liked to sometimes. "You're still my baby."

But that wasn't what Yank was worried about. Hands Down was a thief and a liar. He had hepatitis. He carried a switchblade. He wore cologne that smelled like MD 20/20. He had a prune where most men carried a heart. He wore a locket filled with their dead dog's blood. Whenever he had a hard-on he poked it in Yank's back like it was an old-timey stick-up.

His mother went away. Yank looked back at the Royal but it was useless. The story had died. Hands Down had killed it. The way he killed everything.

Yank stared at the picture of the Mick for what seemed like an hour. He loosed his story from the typewriter and ripped it into little pieces.

When the doorbell rang, he was hunched over in his chair. His mother answered and was overjoyed to see Cousin Eugene and Hands Down. She brought them into the living room and poured vermouths. Hands Down put his hand on Yank's shoulder and said something about being blood and then he laughed. Yank looked at his brother and showed teeth. He remembered what Doc had said. Hands Down didn't own him. He couldn't just paw at him like that.

"Little Brother's got a mean face on," Hands Down said. He sat down and turned on the TV.

Cousin Eugene fiddled around with the rabbit ears until they got a picture going.

"Eight years," Hands Down said. "Still ain't a goddamn thing on the tube."

"Jimmy, *language*," Cousin Eugene said.

"Sorry, Ma," Hands Down said.

His mother shrugged and sipped her vermouth.

Yank got up and turned off the TV. "Leave it off," he said. "We don't put the TV on in the afternoons."

"Well, I'll be," Hands Down said.

"We only put the TV on at night to watch the news and game shows. Rest of the time it stays cold."

Hands Down got up and stood next to Yank. He started dancing around him. "Got into boxing in jail," he said, throwing a couple of punches over Yank's shoulder. "Got pretty good at it too."

"Don't care."

"You still writing stories, Yank? You write any about me?"

"No."

"Sure, you had to. Your big bad brother who treated you like a retard your whole life. Sure you did. Let me see one."

"Leave him alone," Cousin Eugene said.

Yank's face was getting red.

"Let me see one," Hands Down said, and he pulled a punch a couple of inches from Yank's nose. Then he charged past him and made straight for the basement. Yank followed him.

Hands Down took the steps two at a time and pulled up in front of the piano. He reached in and came out with a stack of Yank's stories. He flipped through them. "'Ewing's Boots,'" he said. "Sounds like a real shitpile. 'Butter for the Shifty Bride.' Christ, Yank. What a title! 'Sandra Dee, Your Princess Days Are Over.' 'Christ and Cauliflower.' 'The Wrestlers Who Ran Away.' Where do you come up with this shit?"

Yank swung at Hands Down and connected. Hands Down dropped the stories and laughed. He touched a stitch of blood on his lower lip. "Well, I'll be," he said again. "Little Brother wants to box."

Yank put up his hands. He thought about the picture of the Mick. Hands Down crossed with a right and Yank ducked it.

Cousin Eugene came downstairs as Yank and Hands Down circled each other in front of the broken player piano. "Boys, come on now," he said. "No need to bring it to this."

Yank looked at him. Cousin Eugene had lied about Michigan. He had brought Hands Down back into the house. "You goddamn liar," Yank said.

"Now, Yank."

"Just shut up."

Hands Down thumbed Yank's belly. "You're getting soft, Little Brother. All this sitting around on your ass."

Yank lashed out and connected with a one-two to the side of Hands Down's head. He didn't know that he had that much power in him, but Hands Down went spilling out across the piano, the keys sending out a wrecked sound.

Hands Down came back at him and threw a couple

of wild punches. He landed one and Yank tasted blood between his teeth.

"You don't know what you're doing," Cousin Eugene said.

Hands Down took his switchblade out of his back pocket and fisted it so the blade was poking out between his fingers. He snapped his hand at Yank, missing to the right.

Yank moved in and bear-hugged Hands Down. Hands Down dropped the switchblade. Yank got behind him and slammed his head down on the edge of the piano. Blood sprayed out across the ivory. "He's not coming back into our lives and ruining everything," Yank said.

Cousin Eugene pulled Yank back. "The hell he's not," he said. "He's your brother."

Hands Down was balled up on the floor. Yank was not done. He wanted to kick his brother, wanted to open up his head and see the evil fall out. Cousin Eugene held him back. "Go upstairs now, Yank. Cool down." He pushed him away and bent over Hands Down, asking if he was okay. Hands Down mumbled. Yank turned and went upstairs. He sat down at the Royal and started working on a new story. The truth of the matter was that he had about ten stories where his brother played a part. There was "Dust, Dribble, Drills." In that one, a character called Knuckles—based on Hands Down—got what was coming to him when he tried to hold up a rural bank and ran into a driller killer. In "Shamrock Thompson," an old Irish grouch offed a young thief named Tommy the Sandwich— again modeled on Hands Down—who didn't know how to keep his mouth shut about anything. There were others—"Mad William Whitman," "Train Wreck Blues," "Stink Bottom," "Cans and Cotton," and "Lena the Cutman"—that all had fuck-ups like Hands Down in them, burdens that made the world a worse and heavier place.

Now there was going to be another story. He started typing and he realized that it was the kind of story that people dedicated their whole lives to. Academics in crummy offices wearing beards and birth control glasses puzzled over language this thick and rich. They assigned writing like this to students and said, "Look! Here's how." And this time he was cutting straight to the bone. The main character was called Hands Down and he wasn't a character at all. He was Hands Down himself. He was a bad guy, a bad brother, and—most of all—a sinner on the ropes. The story was pouring out of Yank. It showed Hands Down boxing in a sweaty dark room in Sing Sing. It showed him getting out of prison and going back to his old ways. The Royal was humming. He had three pages piled on the desk when his mother came over and asked about Hands Down. "Not now, Ma," he said. "I'm going good here."

Cousin Eugene and Hands Down came back upstairs soon after. Hands Down's shirt was off and he was holding it over his mouth and nose.

"Fucker broke my nose," Hands Down said. "Knocked out two of my teeth."

Yank stopped typing and looked at his mother. "I did it, Ma. But he deserved it. He's a bad guy. He's always been a bad guy. Remember when we were kids? Remember at Yankee Stadium he tried to push me over the wall in the right field seats? Remember in church he used to fart and say God was shit? Remember the girls he brought here and what they did? Remember he robbed all your jewelry and he took those bonds Dad left you?" It was all going to be in the story. Maybe a book. *Hands Down: The Story of a First-Class Shitheel.*

"I did more than that," Hands Down said. "More than you ever knew. I sold your baseball cards, the ones Mom told you got ruined in the flood downstairs. Your Mantle rookie. And that day you went to Times Square, I got Lucy drunk and ate her out. Your only girlfriend and you never even got to touch her. Her puss tasted like rat poison. Then there was the dog." He held out the locket he wore around his neck. "Mulligan. I hit that little fucker with my car pulling into the driveway. Drunk as shit one afternoon and *thump*. Just tapped him. Hardly even showed on the poor mutt. Blew him up on the inside though. Mom knew. I put his blood in this locket because—shit, why not?" Hands Down took the shirt away from his face. The blood had swished across his cheeks.

Yank started typing again. It was all going in the book. It was going to be a big story about the way death sometimes sits on your chest in the form of a shitty brother.

"I'm not done with you, Little Brother," Hands Down said. He came over and boxed Yank's ear.

Yank stopped typing, stood up, picked up the Royal, and turned on his brother with it. Hands Down caught the carriage arm in the temple and the ribbon popped and unspooled over his shoulders. He hit the floor again. The Royal had opened his head up. He was bleeding from the mouth, from the nose, from the ears, from the deep cut matted under his hair. Yank heard his mother drop her vermouth glass but he didn't look at her. He put his typewriter back on the desk and saw that it was ruined and bloody. He would need a new one. They had a little Olivetti at the typewriter shop on East Tremont that he could probably afford.

Cousin Eugene knelt over Hands Down. "What'd you do, Yank?" he said.

Yank said nothing. He walked over his brother and out the door. He walked to MacDougal's and ordered a double whiskey.

Doc was still there. He could probably tell that something was wrong. He poured the drink and then went over to the phone.

Yank was thinking about the book. How it would end. Hands Down brained with a typewriter by his own brother. It was a beautiful thing to think about. The book was coming together in a strange and glorious way.

POOR BOX

The poor box was pretty well-secured to the floor and it took a good push to get it loose. Everyone turned around in their pews to look at me. Monsignor Ciardi was receiving the gifts from two balding fat women. Even he stopped what he was doing and shot me a dirty look. I half-expected a candle to come flying at my head.

The usher, an old man in a purple jacket, put his hand on my shoulder.

"I dropped my keys in there," I said, and I reached into the box. I had no idea that there were metal teeth in a poor box, and I got scraped up pretty good.

Purple Jacket didn't buy my story of course, and he was a lot more powerful than he looked. He grabbed me from behind and dragged me out the front doors, dropping me in the street. I dusted my jacket and pants off, and I walked away from the place, figuring that my take from the poor box wouldn't have been so hot anyway.

I walked over to Maloney's on West Twelfth Street, figuring I'd try to talk some twist into buying me a beer. I had fantasies about finding women like Faye Dunaway in *Barfly* at places like Maloney's. It wasn't goddamn likely. But I always kept my fingers crossed.

On the walk over I tried not to think about what I'd done in St. Mary's. It was a rotten thing to do, and my mother would have cried in her black coffee if she'd seen it. *Not the way I raised you, Angelo*, she'd say. *Shit, Ma*, I'd say, *give me a goddamn break*. Anyhow, she'd hear about it from Ciardi. They were tight. She'd go in for confession or something and Ciardi would chew her ear off about what a drunken bum I was. I was forty and she was seventy and she was still getting reports from priests about me.

I got to Maloney's, and it was empty. Tommy Rest Stop was bartending. "What can I get you, Ang?" Tommy said, as I took my stool.

"Nothing. I'm broke. Just gonna wait here until some fancy lady buys me a beer."

Tommy shook his head, said nothing.

Next thing I knew a guy walked in, a tall dude with dark hair and sunglasses. He didn't look like he came from the neighborhood. He looked more like Park Slope or Williamsburg. Kind of like a hipster with grease in his hair, blue jeans that looked like he bought them worn out, and a tight blue T-shirt that said *Mordecai Murphy*. He had wormy lips. He sat down at the bar and ordered a pint of Iron City. Iron City was on special, and I'd put back a ton of it in the past few weeks. Drank all my mother's social security money away. Tommy served the guy, and I watched as he took out his wallet and put a five on the bar. Tommy collected it and brought back change. The guy lifted the beer and took a long slug, and then he turned to me and said, "Something I can help you with?"

"Just admiring your beer," I said.

"You hitting me up for a beer, man?"

Showing him my empty pockets, I said, "I'm busted. Payday's tomorrow. How about it? A little charity."

The guy nodded at Tommy, and Tommy pulled me a pint of Iron City. He put it on a coaster in front of me, and it looked like the best goddamn beer in history. The pint glowed, and I wrapped my hands around it just to feel how cold it was. I should've taken it slow, sipped at it and savored it, but instead I gunned it and let a loud belch rip when I was done.

"Nice, Ang," Tommy said.

"Thanks," I said to the guy, ignoring Tommy. "My name's Angelo." I held out my hand.

"Mark," he said, and he shook. He had a real limp handshake and for a second I thought about taking him out in the alley behind Maloney's and rolling him, snagging that wallet out of his tight fifty-dollar jeans.

"Thanks again for the beer, Mark," I said.

"No problem."

We sat there for a while. Mark got up and put a song on the jukebox. It was Merle Haggard's "Carolyn." I thought that it was a strange pick for a little hipster shithead. "Good choice," I said, trying to draw something out of him.

But he just nodded.

The door swung open and three guys walked in. They were greasy gangster-types. They all wore matching maroon sweat suits and gold crosses on heavy gold chains. The biggest guy had a face that looked like rubble. He was the one who spoke first. "Mark," he said. "Mark, Mark, Mark."

Mark looked down into his beer.

"You just walk away from us?"

Mark took a sip of beer.

The guys approached. They looked over at me like I was a big pile of nothing. I noticed that they all had their names sewn onto the right breast pockets of their sweat suit jackets in white curlicue script. The one who had spoken to Mark was called Vito. The other two were called Giovanni and Antonio. Vito was the ringleader. The other two just sat there and looked tough. They had toothpicks in their mouths.

Tommy Rest Stop came over and said, "Can I get you fellas something?"

Vito took the stool next to Mark and put his elbow on his shoulder. "What's our boy here drinking?" he said.

"Iron City. It's on special."

"Make it four Iron Cities."

I said, "How about five, Vito?"

Vito looked at me like *what the fuck*. "And who are you?" he said.

"Angelo," I said. I figured he'd buy it. That he would guess he knew me and just buy the extra beer for the hell of it.

"I know you?"

"Big time."

"Big time, huh? Where from?"

I had to come up with something. "School. Grade school. Way back."

"St. Mary's?"

"Big time." I *had* gone to St. Mary's for grade school, but there was no way I had been there the same time as Vito. He had to be about ten years younger than me.

"You look old," he said.

"Booze," I said.

He turned to Tommy. "All right, get this bum a beer too," he said.

Tommy pulled five beers and set one in front of me and the others in front of Mark and Vito and his two henchmen. I gunned mine like a champ.

Vito looked at me again. "Disgusting," he said.

"Thanks, Vito," I said. "Old time's sake. All that."

He ignored me and turned back to Mark. "So, why'd you run?"

Mark just sat there. He took a long slug of Iron City.

"He's quiet," I said.

"Sure is," Vito said. "You got nothing to say, kid?"

Mark's lip was twitching a little.

"You're after him, huh?" I said. "Something he did."

"Or didn't do."

"Whatever. It's like that Hemingway story 'The Killers.' You ever read it?"

"You calling us killers?"

"No."

"You think we're killers?"

"Not at all."

"You're a big reader, huh? I read, too. Last thing I read was the obituary page this morning."

"I was just saying it's like that story. Where they come into the diner for Ole Andreson. But it's different because Ole's not there. Mark's here. So I guess it's not as good."

"It'll get more interesting, I think," Vito said. "Won't it, Mark?" He messed up Mark's hair. He drew back and looked at the T-shirt he was wearing. "Mordecai Murphy? Fuck's that, a band?"

Mark didn't answer.

"They got any hits?"

Still nothing.

"You wear the shirt, you gotta know the songs. They got any big hits?"

"Nothing you would know," Mark said.

"Nothing I would know, huh?"

"They're on an indie label."

"An indie label, huh? That's fucking great."

Mark lifted his pint and emptied it. "Carolyn" had stopped playing a few minutes before. He got up, went over to the jukebox, and punched in some numbers. Another good choice. Johnny and June Carter Cash doing "Far Side Banks of Jordan."

"One last song," Mark said.

"'One last song,'" Vito said. "I like that."

The song played and it was a real heartbreaker. I thought about my mother again. How she would feel when she found out I'd tried to tip over the poor box.

Vito, Antonio, and Giovanni drank their beers slowly. No way they were going to finish them. As the song played, they seemed to get uncomfortable. I could smell their cologne as they worked up good sweats in the stuffy bar.

The song ended. Mark looked pretty goddamn composed.

Vito said, "Antonio, Giovanni, take the kid out to the car."

Antonio and Giovanni grabbed Mark by the back of his neck and dragged him out the door.

Tommy Rest Stop pretended he hadn't seen anything.

I looked at the three half-full beers the mobsters had left on the bar. In my mind's eye, I saw myself gunning them.

Vito stood up. He walked over to me. "Big smart-ass," he said. "Big smart guy."

I smiled.

"I really know you, smart guy?"

"Maybe," I said. "I went to St. Mary's."

"But you're older, right?"

"A few years."

"A few years? How old are you?"

"Forty."

"Jesus. Forty? You look a hundred."

"Been told."

"I'm twenty-nine. That's eleven years difference."

"Never was good at math."

"I bet. But you're good at being a smart-ass. You're real good at that. You're real good at sticking your nose in where it doesn't belong."

"Been told that, too."

Vito drew back. "You sure mouth off a lot for a goddamn bum." He closed in, grabbed my shoulder, turned me away from the bar and slapped me. It was embarrassing. He didn't even punch me. Just slapped me like I was a whore who had disappointed him.

I looked over to where Tommy had been sitting. He had disappeared back into the kitchen.

Vito said, "You like getting slapped like a bitch? You mouth off like one, you get slapped like one."

"I'm sorry."

"You're a real sissy bum. Don't have enough booze in you to be brave, do you? Couple of more beers I bet you'd be swinging at me."

"No way."

"What's your name?"

"Angelo."

"Angelo what?"

"Angelo Murphy."

"Angelo Murphy? Fuck kind of name is that?"

"Named after my grandfather on my mother's side, but my father's Irish."

"Your mother's a nice old little Italian lady, and your father's a worthless drunken mick, huh? I see where you get it from."

"No need to say that."

Vito laughed. "You're a prize. What'd you see in here tonight, Angelo Murphy?"

"Not a thing. All I see right now are three leftover beers that need finishing."

"That's your Irish blood screaming. You're in deep shit and all you can do is daydream about booze. You got a problem there."

"I'll seek help tomorrow."

"You want our beers?" He went over to the beers and spit into them. Then he pushed them in front of me. "Drink up."

I didn't have to think twice. I sucked them down. The Iron City still tasted good.

"A little part of me feels bad for you," he said. "Something that got stuck in my gut in St. Mary's. Whatever you call it. A little part of me really feels bad about what kind of bum you are. But you shouldn't stick your bum nose where it doesn't belong. That's the mick in you. Makes you nosy. Now I got to take you out to the car."

"I didn't see anything."

"You're gonna cry now, I bet. I seen it a million times. A million bums like you I've seen. Drink up to get brave in your blood. That's all. Not enough booze and you turn sissy. Whimper for your life. Come with me. Don't make me drag you out there."

I got up. I felt unsteady.

"You got big guts now, huh?"

He led me by the arm outside. A white Nissan Altima was waiting at the bus stop across the street. It was running. Mark and Giovanni were in the backseat. Antonio was in the driver's seat. Vito stuck me in the back and got in the passenger side. Giovanni was holding a gun on Mark and now he showed it to me. "Don't say nothing," he said. Mark had his eyes closed. He wouldn't even look at me.

"Smart guy doesn't have such a big goddamn mouth now," Vito said, and he laughed.

"No," Antonio said. "Ain't cracking jokes now, the piece of shit."

"What about the bartender?" Giovanni said. I could feel his hot breath on my face across the backseat. It stunk of garlic.

"He's cool," Vito said. "He's on Joe Gaspipe's payroll."

You son of a bitch, Tommy.

"You don't think he even gives a shit about his buddy here?" Giovanni said.

"Nobody cares about this bum."

"I won't say anything," I said.

Vito said, "Oh, the smart guy speaks." He turned around in his seat. "Giovanni, show the smart guy what happens when he shoots his trap off now."

Giovanni reached across Mark and hit me in the jaw with the butt-end of his gun.

"You see what happens," Vito said. "The bum talks and the bum gets hit. Lesson in this: Shut up, bum."

I nodded. Felt blood running between my teeth.

Antonio pulled the car away from the curb.

Vito turned on the radio. He put on an awful station that played dance music. I wanted to say something about it, but I knew I'd get another crack in the face.

We drove in silence down Bay Parkway. Antonio made a left under the El on Eighty-Sixth Street, and we drove on until we came to Stillwell Avenue. We passed the projects and drove into Coney Island. Across from the Villa Borghese was a salvage yard. A sign on the fence said *One St p Sal age*. Antonio parked the car on the curb outside. Vito got out, closing the door behind him, and stood under the sign. He put a key in the padlock on the fence, opened it, took off the lock, and swung the gates open. Antonio backed the car into the yard. Vito closed the gates behind him, fastening the lock.

I looked at Mark. His eyes were still closed.

Vito came over to the car and rapped on the window. "Take them out, G," he said.

Giovanni waved the gun at me and Mark. "Out," he said.

Mark didn't move.

Giovanni nudged him. "Open your eyes, kid."

Mark finally opened his eyes.

I got out first. Vito grabbed me and led me over to where there were a few rundown cars parked side by side. Giovanni and Antonio, with Mark in tow, were close behind. They pushed Mark down to the ground. "Kneel in front of the Chrysler," Vito said to him.

It was hard to tell which of the cars was a Chrysler. Mark just took a guess, and he kneeled in front of a gray car with a cracked windshield.

"And you kneel in front of the Chevy, bum," Vito said to me.

I kneeled in front of a blue car with the front end smashed in.

"That look like a Chevy to you, smart guy?"

I looked at the car. It looked everything like a Chevy and nothing like a Chevy. I moved over, on my knees, to the next car. It was red and the trunk was open and it had no hood.

"Better," Vito said.

I was one car over from Mark.

"Hey, bum," Vito said. "I got something to show you. I'm gonna show you what happens to guys don't come through. Guys that like money but don't like consequences. Guys that go pussy when it counts. Guys that betray you."

I looked over at Mark. Vito stepped up behind him,

a gun in his hand. He pressed the gun against the back of Mark's head. He pulled the trigger and there was a swampy spray of blood. I was hit with some of it, and I turned away. Mark was down on the ground, his head bulleted open. I collapsed to my hands and puked.

"Looks like the bum doesn't like bloodshed," Vito said.

"Looks like it," Antonio said.

Vito said, "What have an Irishman and Jesus Christ got in common?"

"I don't know," Antonio said.

"I don't know, V. What?" Giovanni said.

"They both lived at home with their mothers until they were thirty-three and neither had a job."

Antonio and Giovanni let loose laughing.

"Except this bum's forty. Still lives at home with his mother, I bet. Don't you?"

I nodded.

"What's that? You nodding your head down there? Watch out you don't get puke all over yourself. So, that's true? You live at home with your mother?"

"I do," I said.

"No job, right?"

"No."

"You just drink. You take whatever money your mother gives you and you drink."

"Yeah."

"Probably don't even do anything nice for her, do you?"

"No."

"She probably wants you to go to church with her and you don't go. Right? Come on, Angelo. It's like confession."

"I don't know," I said.

"Looks like I hit a sore spot."

"Looks like it," Giovanni said.

"You go to church with your nice old mother or not?" Vito said. He came up behind me and pointed the gun at my back.

"Not usually," I said.

"Didn't think so."

"But I go sometimes alone."

"I don't care."

"Tonight I was there alone. I was at St. Mary's."

"I don't care."

"I tried to steal money out of the poor box."

Vito laughed. "He's *confessing*."

"In the middle of Mass."

"Jesus. You're pathetic. Almost too pathetic to shoot. Like one of those wimpy dogs you see out in the rain."

"I got thrown out of church."

"He's got a lot of sins to confess," Giovanni said.

"No shit," Vito said. "What else did you do?"

"Sometimes I steal my mother's social security money."

"She must notice that."

"She does, but she doesn't do anything."

"What else?"

"I pawned her engagement ring."

"Probably wasn't worth much, your father being a drunken paddy."

"It was nice."

"I ain't got all night here. Say a million Our Fathers and a hundred million Hail Marys. Maybe God'll forgive you since you're such a sorry sack of shit." Vito reached down and put the gun against my neck.

"Wait," I said, squirming away. "Don't do it. Please."

"Beg, bum."

Giovanni said, "I got to make it home to give my father his medicine."

"Patience," Vito said.

"Wait," I said again.

"Say your prayers."

I flailed, turned over on my back, and kicked Vito in the gut before he had a chance to fire. The gun jumped out of his hand. He fell back, and I got to my feet. Antonio and Giovanni, guns drawn, charged. I dove behind the Chevy. They both fired and missed, hitting the car. I looked behind me and saw high piles of junked car parts. Beyond that was another tall fence with barbed wire trim that separated the yard from Coney Island Creek.

I took off and got lost in the maze formed by the piles of rusty parts. I could hear Vito screaming off in the distance. He was telling Antonio and Giovanni to follow me.

After a while, I could hear them close behind me. All of them.

Vito said, "That bum kicks like a goddamn mule."

"Don't worry," Antonio said. "We'll find him. Where's he gonna go?"

"Not the point. I got kicked by a bum. Made me drop my gun."

Giovanni said, "But, V, I got to get my father his medicine."

"Shut the fuck up, would you?"

I finally made it out of the maze and got to the fence. The fence was high, and there was the barbed wire at the top. I didn't have time to think. I started to climb. I got to the top, and the barbed wire hooked into my arm and drew blood. I managed to get my jacket off and throw it over the snare of wire. Then I climbed over it and came down the other side. I was on the banks of Coney Island Creek now. I could hear Vito, Antonio, and Giovanni on the other side of the fence.

"Where is he?" Vito said.

"He couldn't have gotten far," Antonio said. "He must still be in here. No way that bum climbed the fence."

"That his jacket up there?" Giovanni said.

"He got over," Antonio said.

Without pause, they fired a few shots at the fence. I ducked and took off up the east bank of the creek. The creek made a sharp turn up ahead, and I left it behind, crawling up a hill and coming out through a dark thicket of bushes onto Stillwell Avenue. I knew Vito, Antonio, and Giovanni wouldn't climb the fence and that they'd be getting into their car to look for me. I didn't know what to do. I figured it would be easier to find me on Stillwell than on the side streets. I ran parallel to Stillwell on Benson. It was dark and quiet. At Twenty-Fourth Avenue, I made a right and headed for the El.

The station was dead. The guy in the booth was sleeping. I hopped the turnstile. I went up to the platform, sat down on a bench, and waited for a train heading to Manhattan. I tried to catch my breath. Instead, I puked again. Just a little bile. A Chinese lady across the tracks, waiting for a train to Coney, looked at me and made a twisted face.

The train came, and I got on. The car was empty.

I looked out the window as we passed over my neighborhood.

I could see the steeple of St. Mary's. I could also see my house. My mother was there sleeping. I wondered if Vito, Antonio, and Giovanni would find out where I lived. All they had to do was go see Tommy Rest Stop. He'd tell them. They wouldn't kill my mother. She'd probably invite them in for coffee and cannoli, and they'd get along swell. Anyhow, I couldn't go back to warn her. They'd kill me. When I got to the city, I figured I would call her.

The train kept on. I fell asleep. I woke up as we were crossing the East River. I got off the train at the Radio City station. I walked upstairs, and I was out on Sixth Avenue. The streets were alive. Not like my neighborhood. I didn't know where I was going. I thought about going to Grand Central and catching a train to Poughkeepsie. I had a cousin who lived up there. He wouldn't be happy to see me, but he would take me in for a few days. Let me crash on his couch. Buy me a few meals. But I didn't have money for the train. I could board, no problem, but the conductor would come around to collect tickets or money and I'd have nothing for him. I'd get booted off the train in Harlem.

I wondered where else I could go. Then it hit me. St.

Patrick's Cathedral.

I crossed over to Madison and walked up to Fiftieth. The cathedral was there. It was glowing in the night. The big bronze doors were closed. I curled up on the steps and tried to sleep. It was cold without my jacket.

I didn't sleep well. At about six a.m., I sat up. I wanted a cup of coffee.

People started to show up for the seven o'clock Mass at about six-thirty. The doors opened, and I went inside with them. It was warm inside the cathedral. I sat at a pew in the back.

I got up and went over to light a candle. There was a place where you were supposed to put the money after you lit the candle. It looked impossible to get into. It was a metal box with a slot.

There were other poor boxes, though. They were scattered throughout the place. I found one back by the door. I stuck my hand in. This one had teeth, too. Just like the one at St. Mary's. Whoever was making these poor boxes was designing them so it was awfully hard for a poor guy to stick his hand in.

People looked at me. They thought I was joking. It probably looked like some kind of stunt: A tramp dips his hand into a poor box, gets stuck, and jerks around. Charlie Chaplin stuff. Harold Lloyd stuff. It was probably goddamn hilarious.

I felt a hand on my shoulder. I turned around. It was a priest. He was dressed in black and wearing his collar. "Son," he said, "you can't get your hand in there. I don't think it's possible."

"I'm sorry, Father," I said.

"Are you stuck?"

"I think so, Father."

He took me by the arm and pulled. I was free. He looked at the part of my arm that had been cut up by the barbed wire.

"You should go to a hospital," he said.

"I'll be okay," I said.

"Mass is going to begin in twenty minutes. Will you stay? We can talk afterward. I'll buy you a coffee."

"Thank you."

"Are you going to be okay?"

"I think so."

"I'll pray for you."

"I've done a lot wrong. I have a lot to confess."

"We're all sinners."

"I know."

He extended his hand. "I'm Father Timothy."

"Angelo Murphy," I said, and I shook on it.

"I'll meet you on the front steps at eight-thirty, Angelo." Father Timothy walked away. I sat down in a nearby pew.

The Mass was very nice. Father Timothy said it. He was wearing his big robes now. I remembered how, when I was a kid, I used to wish that you could know who was saying a Mass like you could know who was pitching a ballgame. That way, you could always catch the priest you wanted to hear. Father Timothy was good. He would have been my number one.

After Mass, at a little after eight-thirty, true to his word, Father Timothy met me on the front steps. He was wearing a Navy pea coat. I could still see his collar peeking out.

We walked over to a deli on Fifty-First Street. He

bought us both coffees, and we sat down at a booth up front by the counter. Father Timothy took off his coat.

"You're having problems, I take it?" Father Timothy said.

"Big time," I said.

"What is it?"

"First, I need to call my mother. Make sure she's okay."

"Go ahead. I think there's a payphone by the restroom."

"Do you have fifty cents I can borrow?"

Father Timothy dug around in his pocket and gave me a quarter, two dimes, and a nickel. I went over to the phone, which was nestled in a small nook at the back of the deli, and I dialed my mother's number. No answer. I was worried. She could be at Mass herself, but she usually went to the ten o'clock in Italian. She had no answering machine. The phone just rang and rang. After a while, I hung up.

I went back to the table and gave Father Timothy back his fifty cents.

"Not there," I said. "I'm very worried."

"What's happened?"

"I don't know. I saw something last night, and some men are after me. I ran. Now I think they're after my mother."

"Have you called the police?"

"No. I've been a bad son too. A bad guy all around. And I can't stop being one. I tried to rob the poor box this morning, and I tried last night at my church in Brooklyn."

"You need to decide that you're not going to do the

wrong things. It's hard sometimes, but that's what it is to be human. But these men . . ."

"I was almost killed last night. I confessed my sins to the man who was going to kill me. Inside, I felt like I had changed. I haven't changed."

"You're going through some dark times. I think you should think about these men who are after you. I think you should call the police."

"Yes, Father."

"Do you want me to call them for you?"

"Yes, Father."

"Okay." Father Timothy got up and went over to the payphone.

I reached across the table and grabbed his jacket. I went through the pockets. I found a pack of cigarettes and his wallet. I opened the wallet. Forty bucks inside. I put the wallet and the cigarettes back in the pocket, and then I stood up. I slipped into the jacket. A perfect fit. I bolted from the place. I looked back only once, as I rounded the corner, and I saw Father Timothy start out the front door, looking to see where I had gone.

I went straight to Grand Central and bought a one-way ticket to Poughkeepsie. My cousin wouldn't be happy to see me, but he was too nice of a guy not to let me stay. I would call my mother again when I got there.

The train didn't leave for a half-hour. I still had some money left, and I bought a short dog of wine at a liquor store next door to Grand Central. I went back and waited for the train. The cars on Metro North trains all had names. I boarded one called the *Thomas Wolfe* and sat in the front of the car. The train left on schedule.

Death Don't Have No Mercy

The conductor took my ticket at the first stop. By then, I had opened the wine and taken a couple of slugs, and I felt pretty good.

ZERO AT THE BONE

"Don't listen to them, Clip," the old cut man said.

"Got to listen. They're right. He beat me here. If he had beat me over there, it'd be different. But he beat me here. I got to listen, Willie."

"You fought your best. I was there. It's not he's a better fighter. Just you were slow tonight. The Scotsman got lucky."

"Slow?"

"Slow."

"Three goddamn rounds. I didn't even get a punch off in the third. He was too fast. Had me tied up."

"Ref stopped the fight too early. You weren't even hurt."

"I felt like about a pound of shit."

"Don't talk down."

"I'm nothing."

"There's still Giles. And Deen. You'll work your way back up to Guthrie. I guarantee it. December. January. You'll be ready by then."

"Yeah," Tommy said. He took the tape off of his hands and massaged his raw knuckles. He had thrown seventy punches and only landed ten. One had been a good jab to Guthrie's face. That was in the first round. Almost all of Tommy's landed punches had come in the first round. In the second, Guthrie had overpowered him and run him ragged. In the third, Guthrie had shut him down completely. The old cut man was trying to convince him that he had fought his best, but he hadn't. It had been ugly, and Tommy didn't care. The truth was he was sorry the referee had stopped the fight so early. He was hoping that Guthrie knocked him out cold and he woke up the next day in a hospital somewhere with a doe-eyed nurse hovering over him. It wasn't happening that way, though. He was leaving the Coliseum quietly through a service exit. Just him and Willie the cut man. His trainer—who was also his old man—was meeting them out back with the car.

They got in the car—Tommy in the front, Willie in the back—and his old man turned and put a hand on Tommy's shoulder. "Don't worry, kiddo. You did okay."

"Okay?" Tommy said.

"Okay. The Scotsman's too fast for you, that's all. We'll work on it. You'll figure out a way. Chin up, Clip."

Tommy couldn't listen to the shit anymore. *You gave it your best shot. Chin up. Get him next time.* He wanted to be back in his apartment, staring at the wall. To hell with the heavybag. To hell with running. To hell with working out. To hell with all the fighters he had ever wanted to be like. To hell with his old man. Tommy was done.

"Clip, you look like you got the weight of the world on your shoulders," his old man said, starting the car and taking them away from the Coliseum. "You got nothing to be ashamed of. Every fighter gets his ass handed to him a few times."

Willie the cut man lit a cigarillo in the back and filled the car up with thick smoke. Tommy rolled down the window.

"You think you had a better shot with Ferranti?" his old man said.

Ferranti had been his trainer for three years, but he had left to work with Bernie Rodriguez in Queens. Tommy had hired on his old man out of desperation. There had been no one else. "It's not that, Pa," Tommy said.

"I know I'm smalltime, kiddo."

"You're a good trainer. Ferranti was washed up." He was lying to his old man. Ferranti was the best. Tommy had been twenty-three and three under Ferranti. With nine KOs. The big guns had all been talking about Tommy "The Clipper" Fitzgerald as a contender. He was even on the undercard at a Mackey-Sorensen bout at Madison Square Garden. With his old man as his trainer, he had one win and five losses. But that wasn't the whole story. It wasn't just his old man. The fire had gone all the way out of him since Ferranti had walked.

They dropped him outside of his apartment, telling him again not to worry about anything. Tommy nodded and said goodbye to his old man and Willie. He stopped at the corner store and bought *The Daily News*. The guy behind the counter looked at him and shook his head.

He went up to his apartment and looked at himself in the small mirror on the wall in the kitchen. His chin was bruised, soft to the touch, but that was it. Guthrie hadn't hurt him all that bad. He cracked a cold beer, sat down on the couch, and flipped through the newspaper. The stories seemed to go through him. There was a big piece on Sorensen organizing a charity bout to raise dough for an orphanage. *Read all about it: Sorensen's a goddamn saint.*

After a while, Tommy decided to go to Casey's. He was pretty sure Sally Unitas would be bartending. Sally was about the only person he wanted to see. She was always good for a laugh. She had big knockers that were always popping out when she bent over to get beers out of the cooler.

When he got to Casey's, he was sad to see Bald Nick behind the bar. Bald Nick never shut up. He talked through the butt end of a cigar and sweated like a hairy wrestler in an old B-movie.

"Clip," Bald Nick said. "Bad damn luck. But things are looking up. Bald Nick's pouring. Forget all your troubles. Bald Nick is pouring tonight, Clip."

Tommy ordered a beer and sat there. Bald Nick put the beer on a green coaster in front of him, and Tommy got to thinking about how it would be nice to take a woman home. Some nights he just wanted to be alone. Other nights he wanted to find a woman to take home. Tonight was one of those nights. He looked across the bar. There was Emily Vincente. She was married. He had made it with her once and vowed he would never sink that low again. There was also Edna. Nobody knew Edna's last name, but she was a pretty mean lay when she wasn't liquored up like a nun on leave. And there was Ginny Carter, who looked to be paired up already with Mikey Elizondo. At the back of the bar, though, Tommy noticed someone new. She was sitting alone at a corner booth, fingering the rim of her beer bottle. Her hair was platinum blonde, and she was pretty in a slutty yet saintly sort of way. There was one thing about her that set her apart from the other women in the bar. She had one arm. One long right arm poking out of a red blouse. Where the left arm should have been, there was nothing. Just space. The sleeve of the blouse was pinned up on that side. The fact that she was missing an arm made her more appealing to Tommy. He ordered a shot of bourbon and two beers. He downed the shot and then carried the beers over to her. "I'm Tommy," he said.

She said, "My name's Reilly."

"Reilly?"

"Reilly."

"That's nice."

"Thanks."

"I bought you a beer. You mind if I sit down?"

"Thanks. Go ahead."

Tommy settled in across from her.

"What do you do, Tommy?" she said.

"I'm a fighter."

"Fancy."

"Turns out I'm no good at it."

"I'm a dental hygienist," she said.

"Isn't that tough with only one wing?"

"I manage."

"It's pretty sexy," he said.

"What?"

"The thought of you cleaning teeth with just the one arm."

She laughed. "You're something."

"Let's finish these beers and get out of here," Tommy said.

"Okay," Reilly said. "I'll take a chance."

Later, sitting on the couch in his living room still wearing most of their clothes, Tommy reached out, unpinned Reilly's left sleeve, and touched the stump. He expected it to be hard and sharp, but it was soft.

"So, how'd you lose it?" Tommy said.

"In the war."

"What war?"

"Kidding. In a car accident."

"It's really something." The stump fascinated him. He traced his finger from the bottom of the stump up to her shoulder.

"It doesn't make you sick?" Reilly said.

"No way."

"A lot of guys, it makes them sick."

"Sure, I guess. But I'm in love with it."

"That's nice."

"It really is something."

"Thanks."

"Listen."

"What?"

"I'm in love with you."

"You've known me an hour."

"I'm nuts."

"You're punchy, that's what it is."

He went over and got a bottle of Irish whiskey out from under the sink. He took a long drink. "I'm not."

"You are."

"Marry me, Reilly." He sat back down next to her.

"You don't know the first thing about me."

"I lost my fight tonight. And I'm in love with you. That's all. Now I'm in the mood to get married."

"You're just in love with my stump."

"That too."

"Hell."

"Marry me."

"We've known each other about an hour. And you only want to get married because you lost and you're drunk."

"I always lose now, and I'm always drunk. Take a chance."

"You're definitely punchy." She laughed. "I could have the clap. Or cancer. Or twelve kids."

"I don't care if you have cancer of the clap. Or herpes of the kids. That stump trumps everything."

"You're sick."

"Maybe."

"And punchy."

"Sure."

She lit a cigarette. It fascinated Tommy, the way she did it all with just the one arm. "You have any music?" she said.

"I have some old country and blues."

"I don't like any of that."

"What do you like?"

"I like classical music."

"When are we gonna get married?"

"Soon, Tommy."

"When are you gonna clean my teeth?"

"Whenever you want. I'll slip you in the back door. Doctor Andersen doesn't need to know. Let me see your teeth."

Tommy opened his mouth, and Reilly looked inside.

"Jesus," Reilly said. "Don't you brush or anything?"

"Sometimes I brush with my finger."

"You don't floss?"

"I use toothpicks."

"I'm gonna clean your teeth."

"You make it sound sexy."

"It can be."

"God, you're the best."

She laughed.

"Listen," he said. "Do you have a car?"

"Yeah, why?"

"Let's go for a ride."

"I don't think so."

He downed the rest of the whiskey.

"It's not a good idea," she said.

"Reilly, we've got to do it. Let's drive to Orchard Beach."

"Not now, Tommy."

He went over to the sink and looked in the cabinet for more whiskey. He found a pint of Seagram's hidden under a pot. He took it out and held it up. "Let's go, Reilly."

Reilly had parked her car on Logan. They walked there. Tommy got under the wheel of the car and turned the radio on. He had the pint of whiskey in his lap. Reilly, sitting crookedly in the passenger seat, had her head in her hand. Tommy fiddled with the radio knob and cursed when he slipped past the station he wanted. He finally found it.

"Can you make it lower?" Reilly said over the music.

Tommy turned the volume down. He put the car in gear and took it away from the curb. It was late, and the streets were quiet. "Classical," Tommy said. "I can't get over it." He felt good, but he also felt terrible. He took a slug of whiskey. He liked Reilly. He liked her very much. He liked his old man too. And, once, he had liked fighting. He almost remembered what it was like. He remembered, as a kid, keeping clippings on his favorite fighters. A shoebox full of them. He had liked that. He would take out the box and read the clippings over and over. He also used to enjoy his long morning runs to Orchard Beach. Back when it was new to him.

They approached Orchard Beach. "I run here every morning," Tommy said. "This is where I go."

Reilly, more relaxed now, said, "I've got places like that."

Tommy parked in a dark corner of the lot next to a tree. He left the lights and the radio on, and he got out from under the wheel. "Come on," he said.

There was a picnic table under the tree. Tommy sat down on the bench.

Reilly got out of the car and sat next to him. She lit a cigarette.

"I sit at this table every morning," he said. "I take a long break. I just sit here."

Reilly passed him the cigarette. He took a drag.

"You're really something," he said. "The way you work things. Lighting cigarettes. You don't seem to have any problem."

"I've been doing it a long time now. Almost fifteen years."

"And you drive that rig like that without any problems?"

She nodded and exhaled.

"Pretty good."

"I don't think we should be here," Reilly said.

"I know."

"It's dark."

"But we're here."

"I want to go."

"In a little while. Let's just sit here."

"Just for a couple of minutes."

"Okay." He took a long pull of the whiskey. "You don't like me anymore, do you?"

"I like you. I just don't want to be here. I'm nervous."

"You don't want to marry me."

"We'll figure it all out tomorrow."

"Sure. Tomorrow. I guess I was just kidding about all of that anyway."

"I figured that."

He finished the whiskey, stood up on the table and threw the bottle into a distant patch of weeds. It made a loud thump against the hard ground. Tommy sat back down.

"Let's go," Reilly said. "I'll drive." She got up and went over to the driver's side of the car.

"Okay," he said.

Reilly got in the car. She stuck her head out the window and said, "Come on, Tommy."

He got in the car on the passenger side and slumped down.

He fell asleep for a little while. When he woke up, they were passing St. Raymond's Cemetery. There was a bar across from the cemetery that was still open. "Stop," he said.

"What?" Reilly said.

"Pull over."

She yanked the car to the side of the road, kicking up dust. Tommy got out.

"Where are you going?" Reilly said.

"I'll see you tomorrow, kiddo," he said, closing the door.

Reilly drove away. Tommy went over to the bar and had a few shots of bottom rack bourbon. The bartender didn't know him. He was glad. He didn't want to go home. After forty-five minutes, he left the bar and crossed the street. He climbed over the cemetery gate. He walked deep into the cemetery and sat down at the base of a tombstone that said something about the dead guy falling asleep in Jesus. This made Tommy angry. He tried to kick the tombstone over, but it wouldn't budge. He left the cemetery and went back to the bar. "You got a payphone here?" he said to the bartender.

The bartender shook his head.

Tommy thought about how no one had payphones anymore. He thought it was sad. "House phone?" Tommy said.

The bartender sighed. "Local?"

Tommy nodded.

He got the phone from under the bar and handed it to Tommy. "Keep it short."

Tommy called his old man and asked him for a ride. His old man said he'd be right over. Tommy hung up the phone and ordered a double shot of bourbon with a beer back. The bartender poured. Tommy emptied his pockets on the bar.

Ten minutes later, his old man showed up. He was wearing sweatpants and a heavy coat. "Pa!" Tommy said. "Have a goddamn drink."

His old man sat next to him at the bar and ordered a glass of beer.

"Take me to the fuckin bridge, Pa," he said and laughed. "I'm gonna jump." He ordered another drink.

"I'll say a prayer for you, Tommy," his old man said. "All I can do."

"Pray up a storm."

They sat at the bar for a while longer, and Tommy's old man bought him a round. When they left, Tommy got into the backseat of his old man's car. "Driver," he said, "take me anywhere but here."

They drove around the neighborhood with the radio on. Tommy's old man pointed out the house on Country Club where he grew up. He stopped the car in front of the house. "The people who live there now, they're loaded. They put a pool in the yard. A big addition on the back."

Tommy shrugged.

"We had nothing back then. Eight of us living in the house. Eating oatmeal for breakfast every morning. Potatoes for dinner. I can't even look at a goddamn potato anymore."

"Rough," Tommy said.

"Listen, you're gonna fight again. You're gonna be good again. You're not just gonna be an opponent. I'm working on a fight now for you with Fitzgerald. In Bay Ridge."

Tommy shook his head. His old man started the car and drove away. When they got back to Tommy's place, his old man helped him inside.

The next morning Tommy woke up and saw his old man sleeping on the couch. He drank some tomato juice dosed with Tabasco, black pepper, and chunks of jalapeno and then went for a run.

At Orchard Beach, he sat on the picnic table and thought about Reilly. He thought about going back to Casey's to find her that night. He thought about the fight with Fitzgerald his old man had set up for him. It was a sure loss. Four rounds on Fitzgerald's turf. It was the point he'd come to in his career. He probably wouldn't win again. He'd fight four-rounders on enemy turf and lose the decision every time because home judges would never go against their guy.

He stopped at a bodega for a bagel on the way home. He also bought a pack of Marlboros, a twelve pack of Budweiser, an issue of *Hustler*, and *The Daily News*. When he got home, his old man was gone. Forty dollars was on the kitchen table with a note that said: *Chin up*.

Tommy ate, thumbed through the *Hustler*, got changed, and went to Casey's. Sally Unitas was bartending. She bought him a beer and he watched her as she bent over to pluck it out of the cooler. He went over to the OTB next door and placed a couple of bets. He lost. He went back and bought another beer and watched Sally get it again. He sat there and hoped Reilly would come in.

He sat there for a few hours and drank eight beers, every other one on the arm. He watched the races and then asked Sally to change the channel and put on the Yankee pre-game.

Reilly finally came in and sat down next to him. He bought her a beer. "I apologize," he said. "Got a little too drunk on you."

She smiled.

"Run away with me. Key West. What do you say?"

"Okay, Tommy," she said. "Let's get a table in the back and talk about it."

Tommy ordered a couple of shots of bourbon and a couple more beers and told Sally he was out of cash and needed a line of credit. She said it was no problem. He and Reilly took the drinks to a back table and sat down. "So, shit, let's get serious," Tommy said.

"Let's," Reilly said.

"Key West. Mojitos. Let's do it."

"Let's," she said. "First . . ."

"First what?"

"A proposition."

"Shoot."

"The dentist I work for."

"I'm with you."

"He's got a safe in the office. Keeps ten grand in it."

"Guy's what, a jerk?"

"No, it's just I'm sick of living the way I live. It's just for the money. I got the building alarm code and I think I know where the combination for the safe is."

"Why don't you do it alone? Why bring someone in you gotta worry about splitting the dough with?"

"I can't do it alone. It's easy, but not that easy. Especially with my disability."

"Playing the old disability card, huh?"

"It's a good card."

"I'm in. What the hell. I'd say shake on it, but you drink your beer, kiddo. Let's do the heist and head south. Get conch fritters in Key West. Spend what we steal."

They went straight to the office. Reilly punched in the alarm code and left the lights off when they got inside. She used a little penlight to guide him around some chairs and a desk. She had the penlight in her mouth and was feeling around with her hand.

"I didn't figure you for a thief," Tommy said and laughed.

"I'm no thief," she said.

"You're a goddamn one-armed bandit."

They went into the back office and she turned on the light. There was a guy in there. He was wearing a white coat. The dentist, Tommy figured. It was a frame-up. Had to be.

"Hey, chump," the guy said.

Reilly went over and stood by him. "Sorry, Tommy," she said. "You're sweet. Really."

"You're the dentist?" Tommy said.

The guy grinned big. Had terrible teeth for a dentist. "So, what's the frame?"

"Need a fall guy, that's all."

"Insurance?"

The dentist showed him a stubby little gun. "Pretty much. You've got a partner. Your partner cleans the office out, turns on you. Reilly's here working late, gets knocked out cold. Payday's big. Hundred grand in the safe goes missing. Plus other stuff that's broken, gone. You, you're just a means to end, a loser who gets to play the part of loser."

Tommy laughed. "What I was born for, I guess." He looked at Reilly. "Kiddo, you really are a one-armed bandit." He thought it'd probably be good to get shot, less like a punch, more like an earthquake in his gut.

Reilly said, "Nothing personal."

"Never was much for things working out." Tommy paused. "A dentist. You could do better."

"I've got three cars," the dentist said. "A condo in downtown Brooklyn."

"Beautiful," Tommy said.

"I like it, you knowing what I have, you not having anything."

"Sure you do."

"I feel bad for you."

"You're lucky, that's all."

"Maybe."

The dentist pulled the trigger, and Tommy felt it go in right above his hipbone. He looked at Reilly as he went down face first. Bested by a woman with one arm. His whole life had been about bastards with two arms throwing punches at him and now here was this woman with one arm, teaching him about betrayal and bad goddamn luck. He saw feet moving around him, heard things being lifted. He was pretty sure he wouldn't die. He felt alive. The bullet wasn't lodged in there, he was sure. Soon there would be sirens. But what if he did just bleed out on the floor of the dentist's office? That was too funny to think about. *Read all about it: Tommy Fitzgerald, done wrong, dead at the dentist's. Tommy Fitzgerald, sad sack of shit right to the goddamn end.*

FAR FROM GOD

He had gone to the house in Phoenicia to clear his head. To get things straight. Things had not gone well in Bay Ridge. Rufus had lied. Ganyuk had been waiting for them at the club. But they had got what they had gone there for, even if it meant cutting down a couple of the Russians.

Now he was just sitting there, in the kitchen, with a bottle of Rheingold. He had put on the radio. They were playing "Lost Highway" by Hank Williams. It was one of his favorite songs. He wondered what station was playing it. It was rare these days to have a station play Hank. Now it was all bad rap and bad pop. He took a long pull off the Rheingold and relaxed. Lit a Lucky Strike. Thought about Donna. Her straight black hair. The rocket tattoo above her right tit. The little knife she kept in a holster around her ankle. Her breath on his neck.

There was a knock on the door. He got up and turned down the radio.

Nobody knew about this place. Not Rufus. Not even Donna. He'd contact her sooner or later, but not even she knew about it. Who could it be? Probably just some nosy neighbor. Some goddamn local selling raffle tickets. Something like that. Had to be.

He went to the door. No peephole. "Who's there?" he said.

Long pause. "My name's Sandy," a girl said.

"Who are you?"

"I live up the road," Sandy said. "Next door to Joe Breyer. You know Joe?"

Joe Breyer was the one guy around here he did know. Joe was a mechanic in town at Roach's Garage, and he'd gone there when he was having trouble with his Chevy Nova back when he was up visiting the house in June. He had gotten drunk with Joe at a dive called Peggy's Runway and even told him about the deal with the Russians. He had slipped and felt bad about it later, but he didn't think Joe had any connection with anyone outside of the garage. Anyhow, Joe was a quiet guy. Kept to himself. Drank some. Fixed cars. "I know Joe," he said.

"Are you Pete?"

"I'm Pete."

"Joe Breyer just wanted me to come up to give you something."

"What is it?"

"A present, I guess. It's in a box, and it's all wrapped up."

Pete opened the door. There she was. Sandy. She had a long, slender neck and bright blue eyes. She wore a denim coat with a T-shirt underneath that said *Red*

Pony Bar and Grill and jeans that looked like they had been spray-painted on. "Sandy," Pete said.

"That's me," she said, sticking out her little hand to shake on it.

Pete shook and held on a bit too long. He noticed that Sandy was wearing Converse sneakers. Black ones. Just like he used to have when he was a kid.

"Here you go," Sandy said, handing Pete the package from Joe Breyer. "Joe said it was something you'd need. Said maybe you lost yours. Or had to get rid of it." She paused. "I don't know what any of that means, and I don't know why he wanted me to deliver it."

It did look like a present. It was wrapped up in newspaper and had a bow on top. "Okay," Pete said.

"Joe's sweet, but he can be a weirdo."

"I guess so."

"He drinks cold coffee and warm orange juice."

Sandy just stood there. She must have been about twenty-two or twenty-three. Pete said, "You wanna come in? Have a beer?"

Sandy shrugged. "Nothing happening at my place tonight."

She walked in past him and took a seat at the kitchen table. Pete opened a Rheingold and set it on a coaster in front of her. She took a long drink straight away, and he could see the red rise up in her cheeks.

Pete sat down across from her at the table and crossed his arms. She looked kind of like a girl he'd dated a long time ago. She had great big lips. Pete said, "So, what's your story, Sandy? You live next door to Joe Breyer with who? Your boyfriend? What's your boyfriend do?"

"I live with my husband," Sandy said, and the air

went out of the room.

Pete gunned his Rheingold, got up and got another. "Your husband?"

"My husband Eddie."

"You're young to be married."

"Not that young. Not when there's nothing else to do."

"Good a reason as any to get hitched."

They worked on their beers. "What do you do?" Sandy said. "This place is usually empty. Is it yours? Joe's mentioned you once or twice, but I've never seen you. Said something about you being from Brooklyn."

Pete tensed up. He didn't like to think that Joe had been talking about him.

"It's okay," Sandy said. "You don't have to tell me."

"You can stay and have as many beers as you want, but there's no time for my life history," Pete said.

"Okay by me."

Pete turned the radio back up. They were talking now. He flipped around, trying to find another station. Nothing. Reception wasn't that good at the house. He found his box of CDs on the floor by the front door and put on Willie Nelson's *Phases and Stages*. He thought it was a good album for just sitting there drinking with a strange married woman.

"You like Willie Nelson?" Sandy said.

"Who doesn't?"

"Who else you like?"

"Hank Williams, Johnny Cash, Merle Haggard, Jerry Jeff Walker, Emmylou, Dolly."

"I like Tim McGraw."

"I guess he's not bad."

"That song he sings about his dad?"

"That's pretty good."

"That's got to be my favorite song of all time. Eddie hates it. Eddie likes, like, Eminem."

Pete tried to get a picture in his head of Eddie. Eddie, storming in on them, with his pants down low, a baby blue ball cap cocked sideways on his head. "You got pretty different taste in music there," Pete said.

"I guess." Sandy finished her beer. "You got another one?"

Pete went to the fridge and grabbed her another Rheingold. He twisted off the cap and set it on the coaster in front of her. He was big on coasters.

"I like this CD," she said.

"It's good. Probably his best, except for *Red Headed Stranger*."

"*Red Headed Stranger*, huh? That's kind of like you. You're a red headed stranger. And you've got all those freckles."

"Believe me, I heard it when I was a kid. *Freckle-faced fuck*. Good stuff. And I'm only half-Irish."

Sandy laughed. "I wasn't making fun. Just saying."

"Listen, Sandy, where's Eddie tonight? It's not good to be sitting around with another man's wife."

"Eddie's at work. He works at the Red Pony." She pointed at her shirt. "He's a busboy, you know? Kind of glorious work."

"You work there too?"

"I work at the video store in town. Reel Good Video. It's kind of a cool place. Pay's shitty, but I get free rentals. That kind of thing."

"What kind of movies you like?"

"My favorite is *Key Largo*. When Frank McCloud says, 'When your head says one thing and your whole life says another, your head always loses.' That's the best. And Lauren Bacall—God, I just love her. That voice. I love everything with Bogie and Bacall. You work at a video store, even a shitty one, and you start to find the good stuff eventually. I've worked there since I was sixteen. Took me a while, but when I started seeing movies like *Key Largo* and *Dark Passage*, they just made me feel good. Made me see the world a different way, you know? Eddie doesn't like the kinds of movies I like. I've got to watch them when he's at work. Or when I'm at the store. He likes, like, only *The Terminator* and *The Matrix* and stuff like that. What do you like?"

"I like Westerns. *The Searchers. Once Upon a Time in the West. 3:10 to Yuma*."

Sandy nodded and took a long pull off her beer. "You gonna open that box from Joe Breyer or what?" she said.

Pete looked at it. "No rush."

"Not even the least bit curious?"

Pete had been playing it like he wasn't curious and all genuine curiosity had gone out of him. What could be in the box after all? Motor oil? "No," he finally said. "Are you?"

"I guess, yeah."

"I'll keep you in suspense then."

About an hour later Pete and Sandy were upstairs in the bedroom, and Sandy was showing Pete what she could do. It had all developed pretty quickly. They had about four more beers each. Around beer number five, Sandy got pretty friendly. She started touching Pete on the knee, rubbing his shoulders, saying that Eddie was a big time bum and that she was looking for something else. Pete thought for a second about Donna, but Donna wasn't there and Sandy was, so he thought more about Sandy. Donna was beautiful, but she was getting old. She had wrinkles around her eyes and her hips were squaring out. Sandy was young, and she had a body like he hadn't seen in a long time.

Afterward, stretched on the bare mattress in the bedroom, as they shared a Lucky, Sandy said to him, "Are you staying here, Pete? For a while? Or are you leaving?"

Pete chewed that over. He wasn't really sure. He had planned on staying there until he could get in touch with Donna and get her up to the house without anybody trailing her. And he had thought about staying there with Donna for good after that. But now there was Sandy. "I'm not sure," he said.

"If you are, that's good. I'll be around, and I'll come over whenever I can. If you want. If you're not, if you're leaving, that's even better. I'd get out of here with you right now. I wouldn't even need to pack a bag."

Pete thought about it. He thought about the places he could go. The places he could take Sandy. He didn't have much money, but there was some. Still, there was this house, where he could live for free. The house had been in his family for a hundred years but now he had no family left. There was only him and this house that nobody else knew about. The house had a wood stove, which would be great in the winter, and the only bill he would have to pay would be the electric. He wouldn't even have a phone. "I don't have much money, Sandy. Just enough for food and beer."

Sandy smiled.

After a while, they went back downstairs. The package from Joe Breyer was still unopened on the table. Naked, Pete opened two more beers and put on *American Recordings* by Johnny Cash. "Delia's Gone" came on, and Sandy, sitting at the table with a blanket draped over her shoulders, said, "Come on, Pete, open that package from Joe Breyer."

"Maybe I will," Pete said. "Maybe I won't."

"You're playing games now."

"You're playing the oldest game of them all."

Sandy laughed. "I'm not playing a game."

"That's the worst kind of game. The kind you don't even know you're playing."

"You're just talking like an old movie," Sandy said.

"I guess," Pete said. He went over to where she sat and stripped the blanket from her shoulders. She sat there naked, and it was pretty cold in the house so she had a bad case of goose pimples. Pete kissed that great neck of hers and those great big lips. They slipped to the floor and fucked again. This time Pete was a little rough with her, pinching her breasts and pulling her hair as she came. She seemed to like it. Just like Donna. Donna always liked the rough stuff too.

When they were done, Sandy went into the bathroom and took a shower. It was a long shower, and Pete could hear her singing. She had a pretty nice voice. Pete put his clothes back on and finished his beer. He read the liner notes to *American Recordings*.

Sandy came back out to the kitchen, wearing a

towel. Her hair was dripping wet.

"Feel better?" Pete said.

"I feel great," Sandy said. She went over and kissed him. Her towel dropped. He kissed her breasts and her stomach.

Sandy pulled away. "Let's get out of this place," she said. "I'm desperate."

"Is that all I am?" Pete asked. "A ticket out of here?"

"I like you, Pete. I don't really know you, but I like you. Let's just get the hell out of here. Whether it works out between us or not. Let's just go. What're you gonna do here? Live a quiet life? Drink beer? Chop wood for the stove? I can tell you're not that kind of guy. I can tell you're in trouble. Like you're on the lam."

"Now who's talking like an old movie?"

"Joe mentioned something about it, the line of work you were in."

Pete tensed up again. "Huh."

"I was talking to him the other day. He came into the store. I see him a lot. Talk to him a lot. He knows Eddie. Hates him. I was talking to him, saying how my life was shit, and he told me all about you. Said you'd be coming up here one day soon. Asked me to deliver the package. Maybe he knew you were my way out. Maybe he saw big things for me. Knew we'd like each other. Knew you were the opposite of Eddie. Maybe it was his way of being kind, having me deliver that present." She paused. "Having you open the door on me. You liked me right away, didn't you, Pete?"

"Yeah."

"You're not just a ticket out. You're the right thing at the right time. You've got a car. Let's go."

"I don't think we'll get very far. This isn't an old movie. I'm not a stick-up man. I'm not gonna rob gas stations."

"We'll make it as far as we can. Then we'll stop there and get jobs and an apartment. We can go to Ohio, Pennsylvania, Maine. Wherever. Even Canada."

"We'll probably drive each other crazy."

"Probably."

"When's Eddie get home?"

"At twelve."

"We've got some time," Pete said. "Have another beer."

They had two more beers each, and Sandy became visibly nervous as midnight neared. Pete wondered if she was nervous because she thought Eddie would find out about them or if it was just because she thought she'd never get the hell out of town. Pete calmed her with kisses on the forehead and chin. Sandy responded, and they necked like teenagers at the kitchen table. Pete put on *Night After Night* by Jerry Jeff Walker. Sandy got up and danced with him to "London Homesick Blues" and "Trashy Women."

At about eleven-fifteen Pete said, "To hell with it. Let's go."

They went out to his Chevy Nova. Pete carried the case of leftover beer, his box of CDs, and his backpack full of clothes and cash. Sandy carried the package from Joe Breyer. "You sure you don't need anything from your house?" Pete said.

"Nothing," Sandy said. "I want to leave it all behind."

Pete put the beer, the CDs, and the backpack in the trunk. Sandy held the package from Joe Breyer in her lap. They got in the car, and Pete started it up. The Nova turned over, and they sped away from the house toward the highway. Pete wondered what he was leaving behind. Anyhow, the house would still be there if things didn't work out. And Donna would still be waiting on his call.

Sandy had the idea to go to Montreal. She said she had always heard about how different it was there. How it was kind of like being in France, except you could drive there. Pete wasn't sure if they'd be able to make it over the border without passports, but he thought it was worth a shot. If they were turned away, he figured they could just drive into Vermont and get a cheap hotel around Burlington.

They took back roads to the Thruway. Around Albany, the road split and they headed northeast. It was dark and empty, and Pete was pretty drunk. They drove straight to Montreal, stopping only once at a diner in Plattsburgh to sober up some. Pete had four cups of coffee and a grilled cheese, and Sandy had cherry pie and a vanilla Coke. They crossed the border at five a.m. The border patrol didn't press too hard about passports. Both of them had their licenses, and that was enough. By then, Pete had completely sobered up, and there was nothing to hide. They were just a couple in love headed to Montreal for a few days. Anyhow, maybe that was what they were doing.

Once across the border, Pete stopped at the first

place he saw and exchanged some of his money. The exchange rate was good, and the thousand dollars he had would go a long way. He only changed five hundred of it, figuring he should keep some American money just in case. Sandy waited in the car for him and smoked a Lucky. While inside, he looked out the big front windows of the place and saw Sandy in the front seat of the Nova, exhaling smoke in a long straight line. He couldn't wait to hole up in a hotel room with her.

When he came back out and got in the car, Pete said, "Montreal here we come."

"Watch out," Sandy said.

"We probably can't check into a hotel for a few hours."

"We could just park and walk around. I'm sorry I don't have any money, Pete."

"It's okay. I've got some."

"I could've gone into the house to get some, but there's not much, and I just figured it wasn't worth it. What if Eddie came home? It wouldn't be worth it to ruin this for, like, fifty bucks or something."

"No, it wouldn't." Now that he was sober, Pete still felt the same way about Sandy. That was good. The thought had occurred to him that the first real thing he would feel when the beer wore off was regret. It hadn't happened. Not yet anyway. Pete pulled away from the exchange place. Sandy put her hand on his knee.

* * *

The drive into Montreal was short. Sandy marveled at the highway signs, which were written in French. She thought it was funny that you could go so much faster in Canada. Pete explained the difference between kilometers-per-hour and miles-per-hour. Sandy laughed. "Oh, shit," she said. "I feel like a moron."

They parked in a municipal lot in Old Montreal and walked around. Pete carried his backpack with him. The first place they stopped was a café on rue St-Antoine Ouest. Pete had another coffee and a croissant. Sandy had a café latte and an omelette. They smoked the last of the Luckies and then bought a package of Gauloises rolling tobacco.

After breakfast, they walked over to the basilica of Notre-Dame de Montreal. Pete said he wanted to go inside and check it out.

"Are you religious, Pete?" Sandy said.

"Yeah," Pete said. He thought about the scene in Bay Ridge. How he had come out of the club, stepping over the Russians, blood sprayed on his shirt. How he had opened the door to the bright day (and closed it on the hand of the younger Russian) and looked up Fourth Avenue at St. Patrick's, the church he had gone to as a kid. And how he had crossed himself just then, saying a short, silent prayer.

"I never would've guessed."

"You're not?"

"I mean, I guess a little. I don't go to church or anything, but I believe in God."

"The way a lot of people are, I guess."

They went into the basilica, and Pete blessed himself with holy water. He lit a votive candle and kneeled in front of a painting of St. Marguerite Bourgeoys. He closed his eyes and prayed. He prayed about all the rotten things he had done. Sandy kneeled next to him. Pete opened his eyes. He could tell that Sandy was amazed by the place. He was amazed too. He leaned over to Sandy and said, "This place is something, huh?"

"Never seen anything like it," Sandy said. "The church I went to as a kid was, like, a little shack."

Pete closed his eyes and prayed some more. "My mother's name was Marguerite," he said. "That's why I'm praying here."

"Where was she from?"

"Her family was French-Huguenot. They lived in the Hudson Valley. My father was Boston Irish. He met my mother at FAO Schwarz in Manhattan. They were both shopping for their nieces and nephews."

They went back outside and walked around Old Montreal for a while more. At around one, they went back to the car. They drove up rue St-Denis and stopped at a place called Castel St-Denis to see if any rooms were available. Pete parked the Nova on the street outside, and they went in. The woman behind the counter said that there were vacancies. She spoke English, but not very well. Her name was Marie. Pete asked where she was from. She told him Aix-en-Provence, France. She had come to Montreal to visit her sick sister in the Seventies, she said, and had wound up staying thirty years. Sandy seemed disinterested in Pete and Marie's conversation. Pete said, "Merci," and Marie smiled and handed him a key. He led Sandy by the hand upstairs.

The room was at the end of a long hallway, far from the other rooms. It was very small. There was a television with an eight-inch screen, a double bed, and a simple bathroom. Pete went out to the car to get his backpack, the CDs, the beer, and the package from Joe Breyer. Sandy sat on the bed and waited for him. When he came back into the room, lugging the backpack and boxes, Sandy asked, "Well, are you finally going to open that package from Joe?"

"I guess," Pete said. He set down the backpack and boxes and sat on the bed next to Sandy with the package from Joe Breyer in his hands. "You know," he said, looking over at the box of CDs, "I brought all those damn CDs and forgot about the stereo."

"Poor baby," Sandy said.

Pete tore the paper and bow off the package to reveal a plain white box. He opened it, and there was a small handgun inside. "Did Joe Breyer give you a note or anything?" Pete said. He took out the gun and checked it for bullets. It was loaded.

"Just what I told you earlier. He said it was something you'd need. Said maybe you lost yours or had to get rid of it. You in trouble, Pete? Are people after you? The work you do, did something go wrong?"

Pete looked at her. He thought about Joe Breyer. Maybe Joe was trying to be a friend, showing him he was behind him after he had spilled about the Bay Ridge situation. Maybe he really—honestly—thought he'd need the gun. Or maybe it was something else altogether. Truth was he didn't know the first goddamn thing about Sandy.

"You know, Joe is kind of absent-minded," Sandy said. "Maybe he, like, accidentally put the gun in there."

"Maybe."

"It's definitely weird." Sandy took the gun and fired off a couple of fake shots, making soft shooting noises with her mouth. "Gun," she said, as if she were naming it.

"Well, Joe Breyer's long behind us anyhow." Pete wrapped his arms around Sandy. He leaned over and kissed her on the neck, brushing one hand over her breasts.

Sandy pulled away. "Not now, Pete. I'm tired. Let's take a nap."

Pete looked at her, surprised. "A nap?"

She pointed the gun at him. "It's been a long night."

"Put the goddamn gun down, Sandy."

Sandy laughed and put the gun down on top of the television. They stretched out on the bed. Pete flipped on the television and settled on the Discovery Channel. Sandy fell asleep quickly, curled up on the edge of the bed away from Pete. Pete couldn't sleep. He cracked a Rheingold and rolled a Gauloises. He lit the cigarette with a book of matches he had picked up at the café. He watched *Mythbusters*, and, after that, he watched *Dirty Jobs*.

Sandy woke up about two hours later. She turned to him and smiled. "Hello, Pete," she said.

"Hi, Sandy." Pete moved in to kiss her.

Again, she pulled away.

"What is it now?"

"I don't know, Pete."

"This isn't why I ran away with you, Sandy. So I could get turned down every time I make a move."

"I know."

"What's going on?"

"Pete, you're, like, a really nice guy." She leaned over and kissed him on the nose.

Pete was getting angry. He should have never left the house in the Catskills. It was a stupid thing to do. Sandy was using him, he could tell. He figured now that she would use those getaway sticks of hers the first chance she got. In the end, he was just her ticket out. She knew all along she wanted to get to Montreal. Probably had somebody up here waiting for her. She didn't have to tell him. He knew it. "Okay, Sandy," Pete said, and he stood up. He opened another Rheingold and gunned it. "I wish they had a radio in here," he said. "I could really go for some Merle. 'If We Make It Through December.' You know that one? It's got to be my favorite song."

"I don't know it," Sandy said.

"It's the best."

"Listen, Pete. I'm going to take a shower, okay?" Sandy said.

"You've got plans, huh?"

"What?"

"Big plans."

"What are you saying?"

"Forget it." He felt like swinging on her suddenly. Those great big lips—they had looked so good earlier—glimmered in the soft light of the room and told the story of a woman born to betray.

"Come on."

"You think I'm a goddamn patsy."

"A what?"

"A pushover."

"Don't go diving off the deep end, Pete, huh?"

He felt hot all over, and his hands were shaking. He tasted blood in his mouth, the way he did sometimes when he got upset. Just like it had been with the Russians after he realized Rufus had lied.

"Pete, don't freak out now," Sandy said. She got up and took off her clothes. She went into the bathroom and turned on the shower. Pete watched her dance around naked, tempting him. She came over and kissed him on the nose again. "Pete," she said. "Don't look so blue."

Pete said nothing.

Sandy got into the shower and started to sing. Pete went over and picked up the gun. It was light, and it felt good in his hand. He thought about the way that Sandy had aimed it and fake-fired. It had been sexy. But upsetting too. She had come off like a girl with a plan. She knew how to handle the gun. It fit just right in her little palm. When she had pointed it at him, he felt his guts tighten. It was the kind of thing someone did to loosen you up—to make you think that a loaded gun in your face was funny and that they would never fire it off—before they shoved it under your chin and blew your teeth up through your eyes.

Sandy was singing "Our House" in the shower. She sounded good.

Pete played it all over in his mind. He was nothing but a patsy. He rolled the gun in his hand and checked on the bullets again. He felt a hard anger, the kind that cuts down to the bone.

"Pete," Sandy said through a stream of water. "You like 'Our House'? I love it. And 'Teach Your Children.' My mom used to sing them to me." She launched into

"Teach Your Children."

"Sure," Pete said, and he walked into the bathroom, leading with the gun. He saw the outline of Sandy behind the thin shower curtain. He was in Canada because of her. Because, drunk on beer, he had allowed her to convince him it was a good idea. And it had seemed like one, when they were rumbling in the sack. Even afterward. Then she started to withhold. But it wasn't until he had seen her—only a couple of hours before—with the gun that things had changed all the way. The fucking gun. They had crossed with it. She claimed the package was from Joe Breyer. But it made more sense that the gun was hers. She was a woman with a plan. There was a hot pulse in her, a deep blind thing that Pete feared.

The gun felt cold in Pete's hand, and he took a long hard swallow. Sandy's silhouette shook. He took one last look at her ass and the dark shape it made through the curtain. He fired the gun high and put two in her back. She gasped and slumped down over the edge of the tub, coughing blood. The curtain came down around her.

Pete wiped off the gun and lifted off the top of the toilet tank. He dropped the gun into the water, and it clattered against the rusty bottom of the tank, settling next to a bleach tablet. He replaced the cover and put a vase of fake flowers and a basket of toiletries on top of it.

He went back out to the bedroom and looked around. He picked up his backpack, the box of CDs and the beer, and he went downstairs. Marie wasn't at the counter. He left sixty dollars Canadian for her and walked out of the place. He threw his stuff in the trunk of the Nova, got under the wheel, and punched the gas. He sped away from Castel St-Denis. Sandy. He'd done to her what she was bound to do to him.

He drove back the way they had come. Getting back into the States took a little more time. There was a long line of cars, and he sat there, smoking. As soon as he crossed the border, he stopped at the first place he saw and changed what was left of the five hundred back to American. He bought a fifth of whiskey and a cheeseburger and sat at a picnic table out behind the station. It was cold, but the whiskey cured that. The hamburger was rough and tasted gritty. He threw it out after two bites. He thought about Sandy. How the bullets had ripped into her mid-song. How they had shattered the tiles when they came out the other side. How that final gasp of hers had filled the room. Pete rolled another cigarette and finished the whiskey. He was calming down. He wondered why she had put the gun in the box. Why she didn't just carry it. It was too much to think about anyway. He would have to go see Joe Breyer. Whatever had happened, it was Joe's fault. Son of a bitch was half-a-redneck with no sense of minding his own business.

Pete put out his cigarette on the hard ground and looked down at his hands. They were steady now. He filled up on gas and then he found a payphone and called Donna. She was glad to hear from him. She said she had been thinking a lot about him. He said that was good and imagined taking that knife out of her ankle holster and playing it up the inside of her thigh. She said that she had a present for him, a bottle of

Black Bush. He said that sounded good too. She said she couldn't wait. He told her where the house was, and she said she'd be on the first bus up. He wasn't worried about anybody trailing her. He hung up the phone and got into the Nova. He turned on the radio and fiddled with the knob until he found a country station. Hank was singing "Cool Water." That was good luck: Hank on the radio again. He put the volume all the way up and pulled away from the place. It would be a good drive back to the house, he could tell.

POUGHKEEPSIE

Books got back in early March. He was staying with his mother over on Innis Avenue. I went there to see him. His mother said he wasn't feeling well. I said I just wanted to return some movies he had lent me way back before he left. Which was sort of true. He had let me borrow *Ms. 45* and *They Call Her One Eye* months before he left for Ohio to work for his uncle. I didn't really want to give them back, but I wanted to tell Books about this idea I had. Tompkins over at Milo's Garage had told me Books had been in looking for a job but that Milo wouldn't hire him because he thought Books was fucked up now. I didn't care.

Books's mother let me in and led me downstairs. Books was sitting on a couch with the TV on mute, trying to figure something out on his guitar. He had a Kramer Aerostar shredder and the frets were worn out. It wasn't plugged in. Back in high school, he'd been in a band with Tug and Matty Ryan called Cutthroat City and a little handmade sticker up near the knobs had the letters CC on it.

"Ma," he said. "I told you."

"It's your old friend Connor, Mike," she said.

I went over and put out my hand. Books shook it. "Long time," I said.

Books nodded.

"You look the same," I said. He was wearing a Soundgarden T-shirt that I remembered him wearing all the time our senior year.

"Can I get you anything to drink, Connor?" his mother said.

"A beer'd be great."

"We don't keep beer in the house."

"Nothing then. Thanks."

She went upstairs. I opened my bag and took out the movies.

"You can keep those," Books said.

"You sure?" I put the tapes back in my bag. "You wanna get out of here? Go to Devlin's for a drink?"

"I don't drink anymore."

"You don't drink?" I thought of Books back in senior year, drinking Heaven Hill out of Kelly McGinn's high heel, doing a keg stand on Tug and Matty's deck in his boxers, keeping his jacket lined with airplane-sized bottles of Jameson and Johnnie Walker stolen from the liquor store in Hyde Park where he worked. "How about a show? Scratch Class is in town. I've got some things I need to talk to you about."

"What kind of things?"

"Tompkins told me you were desperate for work. I've got this job lined up. Thought you might want in."

Books ignored me, refusing to look up. He pressed his palm against the strings.

"Think about it, man. I'll give you a call tomorrow. You want, we'll go to the show. Starts at ten. You got a cell?"

"No," Books said.

"I'll call you here."

Books moved his head, something close to a nod. I left.

I was banging this girl named Tracy who worked for a cleaning service. She kept odd hours. I figured I'd go over to her place, see if she wouldn't put a quick lay on me before she drove the van over to the office on Church Street. I got there and she was listening to some Neil Young song I'd never heard. Drinking a beer. She was happy to see me. I'd met her at Devlin's one night and the special thing about her was that she cleaned these houses and she knew all this stuff about the people who lived in them. Like who collected baseball cards. Who had an antique vase. Who had a porno collection or a coin collection or toy trains. Where the ladies kept their dildos. When they were home and when they weren't. The thing that really interested me was that she cleaned a house where these college girls lived over by Eastman Park. Like eight well-to-do college girls. From Vassar or Marist. I always figured that college kids would make great targets. I knew what college was like. I went to Cortland for a year. You left your door unlocked. You left your shit out all over the place. And now kids had these slim computers, iPods, flatscreen TVs. I was over at this dude's place—this dishwasher from Devlin's who went to Marist—the year before, stoned out of my mind, and he had this digital recorder that went for like three hundred bucks. I could've brought that over to Podsie's and pawned the shit out of it.

Tracy asked me what I'd been doing all day. She thought I worked construction. I told her I'd been out at a site. She thought I was a foreman. I told her I'd been overseeing this big project that these guys from Jersey were involved with.

She put back the rest of her beer, got down on all fours, and crawled toward me. We fucked on the floor and she was loud. Her downstairs neighbors banged on the ceiling with a broom. When we were done, I got her talking about the house where the college girls lived. There were a few details I needed solidified before I tried to talk Books into hitting the house with me. Tracy had told me that all of the girls were going out of town on a retreat for the weekend. I needed to know for sure that *all* of them were going to be gone, that one of them wasn't shacking up with her boyfriend in town. If the house was clear, I figured we'd go for it. Break a basement window. Whatever. Tracy was always saying she couldn't believe the girls lived the way they did, this day and age. No alarm. She told me she was sure the girls would be gone and it was crazy to think of that big house all empty like that. Tracy would probably finger me for the job, but that was no problem. I knew what she liked. I kept her in it, she'd be quiet. Plus I was thinking maybe Books and I would hit the road. Go to Montreal. There was a place there I'd read about, a diner where all of the waitresses were topless.

After Tracy left for work, I sat around and drank her beer and listened to Neil Young. I started thinking about Books and if he would go for it. I wanted to call him up and tell him to quit moping around. I wanted to tell him that there were college girls with dresser drawers full of panties and powders and rings and necklaces, with bookcases full of textbooks and manuals and probably secret photo albums where they'd taken Polaroids of their snatches from funny angles so they could inspect them on the sly, with CD racks full of stuff we could sell at Rhino and Jack's in New Paltz or at a record store in Montreal. I wanted him to have a beer with me and picture these girls. Tight sweaters. Jeans. Purses and hair. Lipstick. *Goddamn, Books*, I wanted to say. *Just goddamn you sorry sack of shit, let's do it.*

But I held off. I went to Devlin's and ordered a double shot of Jack. Reilly was bartending. I told him a Mexican joke Tompkins had said to me. I fucked it up. He didn't laugh. He said his mother was half-Mexican. I figured he was joking. I went home and watched infomercials until I fell asleep.

Next day, I waited until around four to call Books. His mother answered and put him on. I said, "Books, it's me. Con."

"I know."

"You want to go to that show later, talk things over?"

Silence.

"Come on, Books," I said.

"Fine," he said.

I picked him up at nine-thirty and we drove over to the Brass Pail on North Clinton. I lit a joint and offered him some. He shook his head. "Your car's a piece of shit," he said. Other than that, we hardly talked. We just listened to *Dirt*. I turned the volume all the way up on "Rooster." Books looked through my shoebox of cassettes. It was a nice night. I was waiting for a good time to bring up the house. Way I figured it was we could go over there after the show. Around two or three. That way, we could be out before dawn.

We got to the bar and I ordered a Bud and a shot of Jack. Books got a grapefruit juice and the bartender poured it out of one of those sad little cans that you opened by peeling back a sticker.

Books stood in the corner and watched the Vassar girls as they came in. I told him about Tracy. I asked if he was banging anybody. He shook his head.

The opening act was a local band called The Flesh and Blood Show. They were all fat and they thrashed around on the stage. I was pretty sure that the drummer worked in the Home Depot out on Route 9. About ten minutes into their set, I told Books I was going outside. He didn't come with me.

I stood in the alley next to the bar and smoked another joint. Some of the Vassar girls were out there talking about bands I'd never heard of. One of them—a skinny girl with a tattooed neck who reeked of sandalwood—came over and asked me for a pull. Then her friends came over and begged for a hit. By the time the joint made it back around it had been smoked down to the fingers. The girls pretended to be interested in me and then they went back inside. I flicked the joint away and followed them.

Books was at the bar, drinking a double shot of Wild Turkey.

"Fuck happened?" I said.

"Thirsty," he said. He pounded it and ordered another one.

"That a boy," I said.

The Flesh and Blood Show finished and people crowded up to the stage as roadies moved amps and guitars. Books and I stayed back at the bar and kept drinking. I figured it was a good time to bring up the college girls and their big empty house. When I was done talking—done explaining that it would be an easy mark—Books lifted his shirt and showed me the handle of a gun. I didn't know shit about guns. "Christ, Books," I said. The bartender brought back another double Wild Turkey and Books threw it back.

Scratch Class came out and the crowd got loud. There were lots of guys like us there—guys who had grown up listening to Scratch Class, Alice in Chains, Nirvana, Soundgarden—and they were hollering for "Welts." Scratch Class started playing "Fuck Me Off" instead and the crowd went apeshit. Books banged his fist on the bar and sang along. Next they played "The Bride is Candy." Books jumped up and down.

I ordered another beer. A couple of the Vassar girls I'd smoked out came up, asking for more. They weren't interested in the show. I told them I didn't have any. And I wasn't a goddamn dealer. I wanted to listen.

Books was bopping his head, eyes filmy.

It made me think of being in Lenny Cardinale's basement with Books and the Ryan brothers, getting high and playing Super Nintendo, listening to "Welts" over and over. I remembered Books saying how he'd learned the parts. It was strange suddenly that so many years had passed and now Scratch Class—older and one of the only bands from that time still together and still all alive—was playing in Poughkeepsie. We used to complain that bands we loved never came through town. Occasionally there was a good show at The Chance, but the bands we wanted to see always played down in the city.

After the show, we sat out in my car for a while and talked things through. We shared a joint and listened to Side B of *Dirt*. I asked Books about the gun. He said it was just a piece he'd picked up at a gun shop in Ohio after running the table over at this pool hall where he hung out. It was a Taurus 2 inch .38, he said. The guy at the gun shop had sold it to him for a hundred and ninety bucks. I told him we probably wouldn't need it.

"Let's do it now," he said.

"You sure?"

"I'm sure."

I told Books about Montreal. I said we could be there in a few hours. I told him about the topless breakfast joint. He turned the volume up. It was like the old Books.

We drove over to Eastman Park and looked for the house. We found it—a big job that needed new paint—and I circled the block and came back with my lights off. I parked across the street a few houses down in front of a yard that was busy with trees and shrubs. "You want, we can wait until tomorrow night," I said.

"Now," Books said.

We got out of the car and I grabbed a duffel bag and a flashlight from the trunk.

The house had good tree cover, and we went around back and disappeared from sight. I put the duffel bag over my hand and broke out a half-submerged basement window. I climbed in first. Books followed.

The basement was dark. All I could see was a washing machine in the corner. I turned on the flashlight and led the way upstairs. Books looked around. He took a few things—a stubby jar of pennies, an old TV tube, a screwdriver—and put them in the bag.

The door at the top of the stairs wasn't locked.

"Ready?" I said.

Books nodded.

I opened the door and we came out in a kitchen that smelled like vanilla. The light was on over the stove and boxes of Special K lined the top of the refrigerator. Out in the living room, a big screen TV hung from the wall over a table piled high with DVDs. I sat down and looked through the DVDs. *13 Going on 30. The Sound of Music. Annie.* I took what I thought I'd be able to sell. Books went upstairs.

A small dresser squatted in the corner of the room. I went over and looked through the drawers. I found a half-carton of cigarettes, a deck of cards, matches, mittens, a needle and thread, and some fashion magazines. I took the cigarettes and left the rest. Then I followed Books upstairs.

He was sitting on an unmade bed in the room at the end of the hall. Everything in the room made it look like a college girl lived there. A stereo was propped on a cinderblock under a Bjork poster. A few crates of CDs and records were pushed up against the closet. DVDs were out of their cases, scattered on the floor.

Piles of clothes towered around the wicker laundry basket. Books had a stack of records on his lap. He was looking at *Surfer Rosa*. He was holding it up, staring at the picture on the front of the topless girl posing as a flamenco dancer.

"You okay, Books?" I said.

He nodded and put down *Surfer Rosa*, picking up a worn old copy of *In Utero*.

"What do you wanna do, man?"

"I don't know."

"You wanna leave?"

"No."

"Grab some shit."

Books went over and started to go through the girl's dresser drawers. He found underwear, a diary, and a hairbrush. He found a checkbook and some loose change. He found a Christmas card from the girl's grandmother, ten bucks taped to the inside flap. He pocketed the money. I leaned over the crates of CDs and records and pushed the closet door open. I took out a frilly red dress and threw it next to Books on the bed. I tried to imagine the girl. She had no pictures of herself anywhere. Bras hung from a shelf inside the closet. D cups. I picked out a blue lacy one and held it up against my chest. I showed Books. He shook his head like *don't do that*.

We saw the girl before we heard her. She was coming back from the bathroom, wet hair up in a towel, wearing men's boxers and a black T-shirt that said CASH and had a faded picture of Johnny Cash carrying a guitar. She had earbuds in and a palm-sized iPod in her hand.

She stopped dead when she saw us and tried to turn on her heels. She fell down and dropped the iPod.

Tracy's information had been bad.

"Who are you?" the girl said, yanking out the earbuds.

Books took out the gun and fixed it on her.

She started to scream. I went over and put my hand over her mouth. "Shush," I said. "Just shush up now."

"Get away from her," Books said.

I looked at him. "Take it easy, man."

"Back off," he said.

I looked down at the girl. There was a piss stain blossoming out on her boxers. "I take my hand away, you won't scream, right?"

She shook her head.

I took my hand away and backed up. "Anyone else home?" I said.

She nodded.

Books fired and the bullet split the S and H. It was like a movie with the blood and the T-shirt and the half-naked girl. I knew there was no time. I figured she had been lying but I checked the other rooms anyhow. No one else was home. When I got back, Books was standing over the girl. Some of the records he'd been holding were on top of her. *Surfer Rosa* was streaked with blood. He put the gun back in his waistband.

"We've got to go," I said. "That was loud."

He didn't move.

"Come on, Books." I filled the bag with a few last things. I took the girl's iPod and found her wallet in a knapsack on the floor. She had eighty bucks and a Visa card. Books just stood there and watched. I had to drag him downstairs.

We ran outside and got in my car, throwing the stuff in the back. Lights had come on in a house across the street but there were no sirens yet. I punched the gas.

"Fuck did you do, Books?" I said. I turned the radio down. "She's just a goddamn college girl." I thought about how I'd held her bra up against me.

"Just go," he said.

I drove to the train station, about ten minutes of backstreets downhill, and pulled into a spot beyond the tracks, cutting the lights.

Books sat slumped in the passenger seat, looking like a caved-in scarecrow. He opened the glove compartment and found an old wool hat of mine. He put it on and pulled it over his eyebrows.

"You need to get rid of that piece," I said.

He lifted his ass and took the gun from his waistband, letting it balance on his knee. "Where?"

"Wipe it down first. Then walk down and throw it in the river."

He twirled it around on his knee. "I don't want to dump it." He stopped the gun mid-spin with his palm and then picked it up and pointed it at me. "'You need to get rid of that piece,'" he said in a twerpy voice that was supposed to be me.

I said, "I didn't—"

"Let's go to Podsie's," he said.

"We need to get out of town. Montreal, remember? We'll catch a train in a few hours."

"Podsie's."

"He's not open. Not for a few hours."

"We'll wait."

Books, with that gun on me, looked hollow. I half-expected him to yank the trigger. I half-expected my chest to burst open. "Okay," I said. I backed up and turned out of the train station lot.

He lowered the gun and put it back on his knee and spun it again. It fell into the well under the dash. He left it there.

I took turns slowly, made full stops at intersections, accelerated like an old lady at lights. The whole city, I knew, could be a cover for cops now, and I watched for flashes of blue.

Podsie's was off on a side street near Church, next to Kennedy Fried Chicken and a nudie club called Pumps. An alley ran behind the strip of dark buildings, barely wide enough for a car. I pulled in and cut the engine. Metal at top volume pulsed from Pumps.

"I didn't shoot that girl," Books said. "You shot her."

I looked at him. "Sure," I said.

He picked up my shoebox of cassettes and thumbed through them. One tape from high school stopped him. He read the track list out loud.

"You remember when I made that?" I said. "Matty Ryan's sixteenth. The night Gazel Gilchrist gave you head in front of Tug and Matty's mom."

He dropped the shoebox and picked up the gun. "Just shut up. Let's go in."

"He's not in there."

"Doesn't matter."

We got out of the car and went up to the back door of Podsie's. The painted wood was bright with graffiti: *Chump Killed Sally*; *The Ragheads Stole My Shit*; *Dumps Are Beautiful*. Books tried the knob, but it was locked.

"Gotta be an alarm," I said.

"Not Podsie's," Books said.

"Fuck you want in there? We gotta get out of town."

"Thing I sold. After graduation. I wanna see is it still in there."

"You've been in there since. You don't know?"

"Not with an eye for it, I haven't been."

"What happened in Ohio with your uncle?"

"You're asking me what?"

"Tompkins said Milo said you came back fucked up—"

"I've always been fucked up." Books smiled.

"Not like shoot-a-college-girl fucked up. Old Books never lost his shit like that."

"Nothing happened with my uncle. Ohio was boring." He put the gun on me.

I put my hands up. "Books, take it easy."

"Get the door open."

"How?" I said.

"I don't give a shit. Look for something."

I looked around in the alley and found a wire hanger. I knew you could pick locks with a hanger like this—I'd seen it in movies or read about it or some shit—so I bent the hanger and worked the lock with it. I was expecting a click. I was expecting the door to open. But nothing happened. Fifteen minutes I nudged that hanger into the lock. I was sweating. Books was pacing around. I kept expecting a patrol car to roll up on us.

"Christ," Books said. "You're worthless." He kicked at the door and then fell back, dropping the gun. I think he hurt his leg pretty bad doing it. He was sitting on the floor, biting his lip.

"You okay?" I said. I didn't go for the gun.

"I need a drink," he said.

"Let's just get in the car and drive. You can sleep. We'll get a drink when we wake up. We can stop in Hudson and cool off. Lenny lives there now."

"I fucked up my leg," Books said.

"What do you want in Podsie's, man? It can't be important."

Books stood up. He picked up the gun. He limped close to the door and fired at the lock. I covered my ears and moved back. The wood had splintered around the knob where the bullet hit. The music from Pumps was loud, but a gunshot was a gunshot. Books fired again. Pinged the bolt this time. He huffed and shouldered the door. It still wouldn't budge. I looked over at Pumps. I was expecting a bouncer to duck out the rear. I looked up and down the alley. Cops had to show soon. "Let's go in the front," Books said.

"We can't," I said. "We've been lucky this long."

Books limped out of the alley and went around to the front of Podsie's under a swampy streetlight. I followed him. I was calling his name, but Books just stood back in the street and shot out Podsie's front window. The glass crumbled, the store's name swallowed up by the shatter. An alarm spun into the air. Books was still pulling the trigger when he realized there were no bullets left. He tucked the gun into his waistband and climbed into Podsie's through the broken window and the shrill wall of the alarm.

I ran back to the car and cranked the engine. I threw it in reverse and twisted the car up on the sidewalk in front of Podsie's. I decided I'd wait for one minute. Fuck if I was going to let this guy get caught and pin it all on me. I heard sirens. I counted down the minute in my head. I was pumping the gas, waiting to throw it into drive. Books came out, his leg dragging, and got in. I took off and headed in the opposite direction of the sirens. I knew where they'd be coming from. "What the fuck was that?" I said to him.

Books reached into his jacket and took out a watch. It was nothing special. Just an old pocket watch. Tarnished. Not even ticking. "This my grandfather gave me," he said.

"You're gonna get us locked up, Books, for a fucking watch?"

He held the watch by its chain with one hand and let it spill into his other hand, the chain coiling over the scratched glass.

Now the sirens were trembling through the night. I looked in the mirror and didn't see cruisers yet, but it was only a matter of time. I slammed the brakes and cut the lights and pulled over, angling the car into someone's driveway. I figured we'd have a better chance getting lost on foot. "We've gotta run," I said.

Books didn't say anything.

I threw the door open and then went around to his side and tried to pull him out. "Forget the stuff," I said.

He stayed firm in the seat, his jaw tight.

"Books, come on."

The sirens moved closer. I could see blue lights spinning out in the distance.

I ran as fast as I could down a side street, and then I cut into someone's yard and hopped a fence and then I kept hopping fences and I heard barking dogs and I didn't know where I was anymore. The yard I was in, the house had a fire escape. A ladder that dangled to the ground and zig-zagged up to the third floor. I climbed up and then I was looking through a window into someone's dark bedroom. I stood up on the fire escape railing and reached for the edge of the roof. It was sloped with crusty shingles, but I thought it'd be a good place to hide. I pulled myself up and flattened out on the roof.

The moon was brighter high up like that. I could see pigeon shit streaked on the broken shingles. I scuttled to the street side of the roof. I sat up on my elbows. I was a few houses down the block, but I could still see my car and Books was standing outside on the passenger side with the watch in his hand and three cruisers had pulled up behind him, doors open and lights blazing, the cops out and moving forward with guns drawn. They were yelling for Books to get out and get on the ground. I saw Books reach for his waistband, and I bellied back to the middle of the roof and looked up at the moon. I didn't want to see it happen. I heard the shots fill the night. I heard him hit the pavement. That watch, I figured it rolled under the car. I didn't feel sorry for him. I was glad he wouldn't be able to say my name. Still, it was my car down there. I was thinking they'd be coming for me now. I couldn't hide on a roof the rest of my life.

I thought back to the Books I used to know. One time in high school, he'd thrown his arm around me and called me brother. I remembered how good that had made me feel. When you don't have a brother and someone calls you brother, you feel like all the blood in the world is between you and that person. But the Books that was down in the street wasn't my brother. He wasn't anyone's brother.

All I wanted was to get back to Tracy. I knew I could make her and the cops believe it had all been Books's idea. He was wrong in his head, I'd tell them. Just like Milo had said. Maybe it was Ohio. Maybe something else. I'd say I wished I could go back to right before that girl came out of the bathroom and stopped Books from shooting her. I'd say I only went along because I was scared what he'd do to me if I didn't help him. I'd say I wasn't running from the cops, I was running from Books.

I tried to think about drinking beer and getting pussy, the things you think about when you're calming down. Ambulances burned through the night. More cop cars. I visualized Tracy's pussy, the heart of hair, that little smudge of a smile between her legs. Then I thought about slipping from the roof and getting skewered on a fence.

I'd seen a movie about time travel not that long before. I wished that shit was real. I knew I'd go back a long way. Not just to right before Books shot that college girl. I'd go back to before high school. I'd go back to when I was a kid and all that I cared about was Nintendo and basketball in the schoolyard up the block and getting out of going to church.

I fell asleep to sirens, dreaming of pussy and time machines.

I woke up and the sun was trying to kill me. I rolled around and almost took a flop off the roof. Getting down onto the fire escape was tougher than getting up had been. I landed with a thud, the metal clanging under my feet. The window, which had been so dark the night before, was open now. An old lady was sitting with her elbows on the sill. Her white hair was pulled up in a bun. She had glasses dangling around her neck on a beaded chain and gnarly whiskers under her mouth. "Come in for coffee," she said.

"Me?" I said.

"Anyone else on my fire escape?"

"I don't think so. I'm late for something."

"Have a cup of coffee with me. I won't call the cops. I haven't yet."

I went in and followed her through a bedroom that smelled like mothballs to the kitchen. Coffee perked on the stove and toast crumbs scattered the little Formica table where she told me to sit.

I said, "You live up on the third floor like this, all alone?" She went about a hundred pounds and her dress was covered in lint and her hands were veiny and age-spotted the way old lady hands get. She reminded me of a fireball nun, Sister Bernadette, I had for kindergarten.

"Sure," she said. "Thirty years I'm up here." She went over and poured my coffee and brought it back to me. "Black?"

"Fine."

"I heard you go up there last night. On the roof."

"Why didn't you call the cops?"

"Cops." She waved her hand. "I'll tell you something." She leaned in and whispered. "My husband and I, we used to rob banks. All the way from here to Albany."

"You don't know what I did."

"You killed someone? That girl on the news?"

"No, my friend did that."

"It happens."

"You're the craziest goddamn old lady I've ever met."

"I'm just bored." She paused. "I have a car. I want to rob banks again."

I laughed at the thought of me and this old bag doing bank jobs together. I got up and stretched and said, "I don't think so. Thanks for the coffee." I was about to leave, but then I went back to what she'd said about having a car. It was probably a beautiful early-'80s Buick with twenty-seven miles on it. I thought it would be good to have a car. I looked around for keys and I saw some on a hook by the refrigerator.

I went for the keys and the old lady started talking. She'd been nice to me and hadn't called the cops, she was saying, and now I was going to just take her car. I picked her up and threw her over my shoulder and brought her into the bedroom. I put her in the closet, which wasn't very big, and closed the door on her. She was talking the whole time, saying if her husband was alive and when her nephew finds out about this and what a lousy guy I was. I moved a chair in front of the door and turned on the TV in the corner to drown her out. I started going through her drawers and I found pictures of her husband and a bank book and an envelope of twenties. I pocketed the money. In the kitchen I found a bottle of Dewar's and I made a tuna sandwich on rye with mayo that looked questionable. I also took a bag of chips and a bottle of orange juice before going downstairs.

The car was a 2004 Civic. White. It was parked in the driveway and no one saw me get in. A Civic wasn't what I was expecting, but it had a little over two thousand miles on it and the interior smelled like pine. I turned the radio to 104.3 and they were playing a song I hated. I pulled out and saw that my car was gone. I looked for blood on the street. I didn't see any. I drove. I was thinking about Montreal again—because what if Tracy and the cops didn't believe me?—and I was thinking I just might make it and I just might be the smartest guy around.

IN THE NEIGHBORHOOD

Mullen had returned to the old neighborhood for one reason: the last time he was home he'd hidden two thousand dollars in twenties in a shoebox in the crawlspace of his grandmother's attic.

His grandmother was his only living relative. His mother died from cervical cancer when he was six. His father, who had never really been in the picture, got himself shot in a Newark bar over a seventeen-year-old waitress named Savannah—Mullen had heard the story from Joe Greco's cousin who was a cop in Jersey. Mullen's grandfather, who taught him how to fix cars, had died at a slot machine at the Trump in Atlantic City, slumped over another losing game, a bucket of coins toppled at his feet. His grandfather had taken the bus to Atlantic City twice a week from Bay Parkway. One of Mullen's favorite things had been to see him off, to follow the bus until it swerved onto the Belt on-ramp. He liked to picture his grandfather in Atlantic City: getting buffet lunches, having ditzy waitresses in frilled tops delivering drinks on big floaty trays, their hair done up, cleavage open to their ribs. When his grandfather died, Mullen was seventeen, a senior at Our Lady of the Narrows. He didn't have plans for college but with his grandfather gone he knew he wasn't sticking around Brooklyn. He loved his grandmother, all hundred-and-four desperate pounds of her, but he couldn't stay with her. He saw that leading to a life of buttering her burnt toast and holding her arm on walks to Eighty-Sixth Street. So, with almost nothing—some clothes, about three hundred bucks, and his grandfather's old business card ("Crab Mullen, Mechanic, Kinney Motors, Coney Island Avenue")—he kissed his grandmother's blue-white hair and left town with his buddy Pags. Their aim was California. Beaches. Seventy degree days. Pags was an actor and he thought he might be able to score some commercial work. Mullen just wanted out of Brooklyn. Their car broke down in Cleveland, where they had gone out of their way to stay with a guy Pags knew through his salesman uncle. Mullen thought he might be able to fix the car, a rust-waddled Camry with a broken windshield and no radio, but it was a goner. After a week, Mullen and Pags got into it over money and Mullen went to the Greyhound station and got on the first bus out of town. He wound up in Chicago and stayed at his first rooming house. Since then, it'd been a hundred cities and a hundred rooming houses. Dishwasher jobs. Jobs at Quik Lube and Dipstix. Security gigs patrolling parking lots and malls. More often than not, he'd had no jobs. He spent his days in pool halls and his nights in whatever crappy room he could afford. But they were all the same somehow: torn blinds, soggy mattress, walls that looked like they'd been clawed at.

He'd only been back to Brooklyn once since leaving, the time he'd hidden the money in the crawlspace. He must have been twenty-two then. He knew it was dumb not to take it all—that he'd need it wherever he was going next—but he had a moment of clarity and decided it'd be more useful down the line. He'd come about the money honestly. While cleaning out the basement for his grandmother, he found an envelope full of savings bonds his grandfather had given him as gifts and brought them to the bank to cash in. Never mind the taxes. He was too far off the grid for that to matter much. Cashed in, the bonds came out to a little over four grand. Mullen left two and took two. The rest, about a hundred and fifty bucks, he gave to his grandmother. She looked proud when he gave it to her, like he'd done something a man would do for the first time in his life.

And she still remembered it. Sitting at the table on his first afternoon back over instant coffee and stale donuts, she said, "That time you gave me the money, last time you were home, that was so nice of you."

"It was nothing, Gran." Mullen studied her face. Ten years had made her skin look like beach glass. She had the eyes of a blind woman, blue and beady, even though her sight was still good. She smelled like the Sanka she drank. Her flower-patterned housedress was flimsy, almost worn through to sheerness, and he could see fully the places where she sagged. She had to be what—eighty now?

"It was very thoughtful. I told all the girls at church. 'My Sonny,' I says. 'He takes care of his nana.'"

"It was just the one time."

The kitchen was full of fruit flies that hovered around a tin of candied peaches. His grandmother slurped her coffee and gnawed on a heel of donut, making it soft in her mouth. "These donuts are so hard," she said. "What a shame."

Mullen said, "Just take it slow."

He wasn't sure how long he was going to stay after he retrieved the money. She had a room with a spare bed and it might be nice to lay low for a few days or even a few weeks before leaving for wherever he was going next. He was thinking New Orleans. Hop on the Southern Crescent and escape winter. He'd been to New Orleans once. He'd unloaded trucks for a guy who sounded like he was from The Bronx. He'd had coffee at all-night places and his rooming house wasn't bad despite the roaches.

"You'll be here how long?" his grandmother said, as if reading his mind.

"I don't know. A little while."

"Good. I go to the foot doctor on Friday. You'll come with me."

"Sure, I'll come."

"That's a good boy."

The crawlspace was just as Mullen remembered it: dusty and deep. He found strange things inside. Tennis rackets, though no one in his family had ever played tennis. Blown cathode ray tubes from his grandfather's brief spell as a TV fix-it guy after retiring from Kinney.

A stack of *Archie* comics with the covers torn off. A bicycle bell. Empty bottles of Glenlivet. Notebooks his grandfather had kept detailing his history with scratch-offs. Mullen didn't remember burying the shoebox full of money behind all of this stuff, but he must have. In the next minute his heart started backfiring, as he felt around and was unable to find the shoebox. He knew it couldn't be gone. His grandmother wouldn't climb the steps and get down on her knees to search the crawlspace. But what if she'd had someone over to fix something and he was alone up here? Weren't fake repairmen always conning their way into the homes of old ladies?

His heart settled as his hand found a familiar shape. He pulled out the box, smeared with cobwebs, and set it at his knees. He flicked off the lid and saw the stacks of banded money. The bills looked old, a different shade of green than the new bills in circulation, and less cartoony.

Mullen took a hundred bucks and put the box back, nestling it under the bag of blown tubes.

The streets were icy, and Mullen pulled up the collar on his grandfather's winter coat. Gran had insisted he wear it before going out. He'd left her at home in front of the TV with a small dish of potato chips and the volume turned all the way up on a game show.

To Mullen the old neighborhood hadn't changed. A Laundromat had taken the place of the video store across from his grandmother's house and a nail salon had been squeezed in between Giove's Pizza and Flash Auto. Aside from that, everything was the same. It still felt like the inside of something ugly. Familiar smells pawed at him. Bus fumes. Garbage in the gutter. Burning rubber when guidos spun out. Menthol cigarettes from the junior high girls on the stoop outside the corner apartments.

Claude's on Cropsey used to be the only bar around. Mullen hoped it was still there.

He tried not to think too hard about the last place he'd been (Rochester) and why he had to leave (he was run out by the half-Indian father of his Kodak-employed nineteen-year-old girlfriend), but he could've used a cold case of Genesee on a bench by Lake Ontario. He liked drinking with that cold wind coming in from the lake. He could burn through ten cans and feel nothing but triumphant.

The cold wind that came in from the bay here whistled between buildings and knocked Mullen dopey. He missed the town he didn't want to think about and the Kodak girl and the wind off the lake.

Claude's hadn't left. Flickering neon signs behind the barred front window said *C LD B R* and *P BST* and *OP N*. Mullen pushed in through the heavy door.

The men at the bar looked like construction equipment. One shuddered over a bowl of peanuts and a tallboy of Budweiser like an excavator considering the ground. Another was a backhoe, in both shape and manner, unsteady on his weirdly tiny feet. A long-necked man with a longneck of Coors Light was the crane in the operation, sitting there like a sad giraffe, the bottle dangling from his lips. The last man, who Mullen recognized as Dell Burke from Mr. Hudson's barbershop, was a dump truck, leaning on the bar with his elbows, mouth open.

Big Connie was still the bartender. Mullen guessed she'd been sitting in the same place—on a rickety stool under the poorly-propped black-and-white TV at the corner of the bar—the last time he'd been in at seventeen. He also suspected that she'd been wearing the same thing: a bowling shirt with *Big Connie* stitched in script over the breast pocket and sweat pants, a bleach rag slung over her shoulder. She looked a bit older too, her jaw hanging loose, her bone white hair thinner and stringier, her breasts pillowed low to her waist. One hand cradled a White Russian in a pint glass.

Mullen wondered if she'd remember him. He sat down at the bar.

Big Connie struggled over, dragging her leg. She said, "Get you something?" She had only three teeth that Mullen could see and her mouth made a sound like a boot in mud when she spoke. A sour smell rose from her, pickled breath mixed with dirty milk and bleach.

"Just a Bud," Mullen said.

Big Connie leaned over, one leg in the air, and retrieved a Bud from a cooler that coughed more than hummed. She put it on a cocktail napkin in front of Mullen and said, "Two bucks."

Mullen's Bud was lukewarm. He took a sip and then paid Big Connie, fanning out three crumpled singles on the bar.

The TV was showing WPIX. The news. A big-haired anchor with pouty lips talked about a hold-up in Bed-Stuy. Mullen leaned back on the stool. He thought he might be made to feel out of place by the other men at the bar, but none of them so much as looked at him. And no one spoke.

Mullen drained his beer and ordered another. He watched a cockroach scurry across the bar. Dell Burke made a half-hearted stab at it with his glass of scotch and missed. Big Connie shrugged and swatted the air with her bleach rag. The roach made the wall and was camouflaged.

The last time Mullen was at Claude's, he was with Pags. It was about two weeks before they planned on leaving for the West Coast, and they were celebrating. The fact that Claude's was an old man's bar appealed to Mullen and Pags for some reason. They drank there ironically and punched songs they'd grown to hate—Frank Sinatra, Dean Martin, Bobby Darin—into the jukebox to see the old timers get excited and do drunken little dances. Mullen remembered Pags saying, "This place is just so fucking sad."

Looking around, Mullen could almost see himself at seventeen with Pags at a booth in the back. They might have been talking about their dream of the west or about Pags getting head from Joanne Girardi in her garage or about Mullen's desire for ketchup sandwiches.

It didn't make Mullen sad to think this way. He knew that some people hated to remember being a kid as they got older because they had regrets or could never get back to the things they had then. Not Mullen. He wanted to be old like the men in Claude's. Old and lonesome and shut off. He wasn't even thirty-five, and he felt like he fit right into their ranks.

When the door opened, Mullen didn't glance up. There he was, just another fixture at the bar.

But he had to look when whoever came in sat on the stool next to him and threw an arm across his shoulders. She had to be close to fifty with hair dyed platinum like some bottom-rung Marilyn Monroe impersonator. She wore so much makeup that Mullen guessed she must have sprayed it on with a hose. The base looked like a layer of frosting on her skin. Her lips were painted brown and there were lipstick smudges on her yellow teeth. Her neck betrayed her: the skin there wasn't so heavily made up and it looked like it had been pelted with thousands of small pebbles. She had a lazy eye. She smelled like church. Her tits were pushed up by some unsophisticated wrap that scrunched them together and made her cleavage pruny. The dress she wore was too small. Black and tight, it ended just above her knees. She wore a red sash across her waist that served no purpose except accentuating her fat rolls. Her sheer pantyhose had dozens of inch-long runs. Somewhere in her closet there were no doubt heels to match the skimpy dress, but she wasn't wearing them. She had on black orthopedic shoes, the same kind Mullen's grandmother wore. "Buy me a drink?" she said.

"Sure," Mullen said.

Mullen ordered two Buds from Big Connie, who kept her eyes away from the woman and put both in front of Mullen.

Mullen passed one to the woman, who unfurled her heavy arm from his shoulder. "Bottoms up," he said.

She sucked down half the beer in one pull, leaving the neck of the bottle rimmed brown with lipstick.

"God, that's good," she said. "I've been needing that all day. I work for a jeweler and the whole time today I was thinking, 'Man, a cold beer would be good.'" She stuck out her hand, pudgy, with chipped paint on her low-bitten nails. "I'm Nancy."

"Mullen." He shook hello.

"You look young. Are you even thirty? I've got no business talking to you. But I walked in, and I said, 'I bet that nice young man will buy a lady a drink.'"

"Let's see." He paused. "I guess I'm about thirty-two."

"What, you don't keep track?"

"Never had much reason to."

She leaned close to him. "You like older women? I bet you do."

"Sure. Older women are great."

"How about you buy me another drink—a whiskey this time—and we have some fun tonight?" She made as if she were going to nibble his ear, but then backed away and laughed.

The night went to some very strange places. Mullen did like older women, that wasn't a lie. When he went home with women at all, they were usually older. The nineteen-year-old in Rochester had been an exception. He'd often found himself with barflies and landladies, and—in this way—Nancy was a comfort. She was loud and ugly, as they often were, making a spectacle of herself in order to drink for free, but there was some awful experience that shone through, a wisdom of sorts, that drew Mullen in. His only sustained relationship had been in Iowa City with a secretary named Helen who was forty-five. Mullen was twenty-six at the time, and the way Helen carried herself—perpetually shrug-shouldered, glassy-eyed, defeated—made him feel like he had access to something authentic. Nancy reminded him of Helen, except that she was fat, more horrible in many ways, and what should have been processed immediately as repulsion was somehow processed as attraction.

Mullen and Nancy shot whiskeys and danced, even though the jukebox was unplugged. They swirled around the bar, and the other men avoided them. Big Connie did nothing to dissuade or encourage their antics.

It didn't take much convincing on Nancy's part for Mullen to follow her home.

She made him stop at a bodega and buy a twelve-pack of Heineken.

"You're so young," she kept saying. "I can't believe it."

But he didn't feel young. He'd never felt young.

Nancy lived in the basement of a three-family frame house on Bay Thirty-Eighth Street. The mailbox said *CRUZ* in golden, spirally letters. As she put the key in the door, Mullen took notice of her Sacred Heart Auto League keychain. He hefted the Heineken up on his shoulder. She pressed the door open a bit and then turned to him. "Before we go in," she said, "I need to tell you something."

Husband, Mullen thought.

Nancy continued: "I live with my sister. She won't bother us. I have my own room. It's private."

Mullen shrugged and followed Nancy inside.

Nancy's sister was no ordinary sister. She was a quadriplegic and she was parked in front of the TV in the living room, tubes unfurling in every direction from her twisted head. She was in a reclining wheelchair, her matted hair splayed out behind her head. Mullen didn't know the names of the things that surrounded her. It looked like she was hooked up to an IV drip. Maybe an oxygen tank. She wore a blue hospital gown and had a mask over her mouth and nose. Her skin looked greasy. Mullen didn't know what to say.

"That's Victoria," Nancy said. "She really won't bother us."

"It's okay," Mullen said. "Goddamn."

Nancy rushed him past Victoria and into the bedroom, turning on the light and closing the door behind them. She stepped out of her orthopedic shoes and sat down on the side of the unmade bed. She rolled her stockings off and tossed them in the direction of a hamper in the corner.

The room was a panic of sloppiness. Red and black bras littered the floor. A dresser topped with an army of cat figurines sat with its drawers opens, blouses dangling from the edge of the top drawer. The carpet was shaggy and hadn't been vacuumed in a long time. Mullen smelled pine candles, which made him want to puke. He thought he might not be able to perform with that scent in the air. Moldy coffee cups were piled on the bedside stand next to torn issues of *Redbook*. The wallpapered walls had been pecked by age. Moths skittered around inside the rust-brown lampshade. Piles of mildewy towels were lumped behind Nancy on the bed. The baseboard heaters sizzled, sounded something like clicking teeth, and didn't do much to warm the room. A thick gap under the windowsill seeped cold air.

Mullen sat on the bed next to Nancy and said, "Your sister's what, a vegetable?"

"She won't bother us," Nancy said.

"She's okay out there?"

"She's fine. Let me turn out the light." She leaned over him and pressed the button that switched the room to darkness. The moths fell silent. He felt her hands on his belt buckle and then she was on her knees in front of him, urging him to sit up so she could work his pants down. She worked his pecker out over the band of his boxers and sucked him sloppily. Her teeth scraped him and her mouth was dry, but he closed his eyes and leaned back into the towels. The mildew overpowered the pine candles and he started to feel better. Mildew was a familiar smell. He pictured Victoria on the other side of the door. When he finished, Nancy almost gagged and then choked down his load.

She reached up next to him and grabbed a towel and then she turned on the light and wiped her mouth. The brown lipstick came off on the towel and he could see the real color of her lips, pale as a pigeon's beak.

"You're so young," she said.

Mullen was suddenly frightened. He hoped she didn't think he would reciprocate by putting his mouth on her old parts. "What can I do for you?" he said, sitting up.

"Just sit there," she said. She went to her closet and dug around on the top shelf. Coming out with a large cigar box, she toppled back to him and dropped to her knees again. Inside the box was a scatter of green tissue paper. Nancy withdrew a pink vibrator that was extraordinarily long and resembled a bear claw. It had two small prongs like branches and was beaded around the shaft. She held the vibrator against her cheek and said, "This is my friend."

"You want me to—"

"I just want you to watch."

And watch Mullen did. It was an acrobatic display, really. Nancy teetered on her knees, starting with one hand under her dress. She threw her head back and moaned, sounding something like a tea kettle before it whistled.

Again, Mullen thought of Victoria.

Taking her dress off over her head was no easy task for Nancy. She put the vibrator down, resting it on a bunched-up bra, and struggled out of the dress. Her shoulders jerked around. She quivered and grunted. Mullen couldn't see her face, the dress covering it, and he studied what was now revealed. She wore a wrap that looked like a sports bra and flower-banded underwear that hugged her waist. Her hips were wide. Lint puffed out of her belly button.

Finally, the dress was removed and cast aside. Nancy stood up and took off the rest. She picked up the bear claw. Naked, she hovered over Mullen.

"What now?" Mullen said.

"Just keep watching. I like that you're watching." She started to work on herself with the vibrator, the pink base bobbing between her legs. Mullen was compelled to focus on her lazy eye. It was glassy and didn't move with the rest of her. When her eyelids snapped shut and her head tilted back, he took in her body. Her tits sagged to the second rung of her ribcage and she had speckled eye-of-god nipples, the kind that looked pushed-in. Her bush was drizzled with gray. He saw the pink in her pulled out and then pushed in again by the beads. The prongs on the vibrator paid attention to all the necessary places. Her knees were dirty and dry. Her ankles seemed to bulge. Her feet were tiny, lumpy with calluses.

She finished with a throaty yell and fell onto him, pushing him back into the towels and tossing the bear claw on the bed. She dragged her breasts over his face, as if she were trying to land them there. "That was good," she said, sighing. "Did you like it?"

"Sure," Mullen said.

"I liked you watching it." She rolled off of him. "Do you want a drink?"

Mullen nodded.

The bottom drawer of the dresser was her liquor cabinet. He saw plastic bottles of scotch and vodka and club soda. She took out a pint of peach schnapps and swigged from it. She threw it to him and he took a long pull.

"You're so goddamn young," she said.

Mullen and Nancy sat with Victoria for a while and watched TV. She didn't seem to be alive to Mullen. Nancy was wearing a nightgown and Mullen was in his boxers. They had finished the peach schnapps and moved to scotch-and-sodas. Mullen watched Victoria's eyes. They were the color of a table in his grandmother's living room, oaky and brown-flecked, and they seemed to tremble. A late-night rerun of some cop show was on TV. He could see what was on the screen reflected in her eyes.

"Has she always been like this?" Mullen said.

"No," Nancy said. "Not always."

"Was it an accident?"

"She got hit by a bus on Eighty-Sixth Street when she was fifteen."

"That's awful."

"Don't stare at her."

Mullen shook his head and stood up. "I'm sorry. Little drunk, I guess."

Nancy went over and took off Victoria's mask, setting it in her lap. Then she stroked her hair. "That's my Vicky," she said. "My sweet little Vicky."

Mullen looked down at the carpet. Nancy speaking to her sister like she was a cat made him wince.

"Come here," Nancy said to him. "Stroke her hair. She likes it."

"I don't know," Mullen said, not looking up.

"It's fine. It's her favorite thing."

Mullen put his scotch-and-soda on the arm of the couch and stood up. He went over and put his palm on Victoria's forehead and then pushed it back through her hair gently. Her skin felt like the top layer on pudding. Her hair was slimy. "There you go," he said.

"She likes that."

Mullen looked for some evidence that this was true, but Victoria's face gave nothing away. "Are you sure?"

"Sure, I'm sure."

He stroked Victoria's head again, and her desperate breathing—which he hadn't noticed until he got close to her—intensified. "I'm upsetting her," he said.

"You're not," Nancy said. "It's like she's purring. Keep going."

Mullen made faster strokes.

"Say something."

He felt a lump in his throat. "Like what?"

"A minute ago you said, 'There you go.' Say something like that. Something soothing."

He took in Victoria's face: her smooth chin tilted up, her swampy mouth, her crooked nose and too-close eyes, her small forehead, thick eyebrows almost connecting with her hairline at the temples, her skin the color of a new penny flattened by a train, and the zits clotted in bursts on her jaw and above her mouth. "It's okay, Victoria," he said. "Everything's going to be okay."

He left Nancy's, taking her number and promising to call. He didn't have a number for her in return, he explained, because he was staying with his grandmother and didn't want to give hers out since every call she received had the potential for catastrophe. He didn't want to be responsible for her rushing to lift the receiver off the hook and stumbling on her way into the kitchen. He wasn't sure if that was true, but it seemed like it would be: old ladies were capable of that kind of nonsense. Anyhow, he'd probably just run into Nancy at Claude's and he could decide then—when he was good and drunk—if he wanted to get up to anything weird with her again. Head was head if you could get it. He knew not to take that much for granted.

The walk home was only a few blocks. At two in the morning, the neighborhood looked gauzy under streetlamps. He almost slipped on dirty ice.

Mullen thought a lot about Victoria. Her face. The way she reclined in that chair. The feel of her hair under his fingers. Petting her had reminded him of lighting candles in church for his grandfather as a high school senior.

He wondered if Nancy ever made Victoria watch her with the vibrator.

Back at his grandmother's house, he opened the door quietly and slipped inside. He checked on her, asleep on the recliner in front of the TV with a checkered blanket tucked up under her chin and a bowl of marshmallows in her lap, and then he went to his old bedroom in the back of the house. Now it was full of junk, piled high with newspapers and Mass cards and pictures of his grandfather and his mother. Thankfully, the bed was still there. He took off his grandfather's jacket and climbed onto it, pushing a few old stuffed bears onto the floor. He put his hands behind his head on the pillow and looked at the ceiling where cracks spun around a water spot. The mattress was caved-in, and the comforter smelled of moth balls. It reminded him of a rooming house he'd stayed at in Toronto once. He kept his eyes open for what seemed like a long time.

In the morning—or was it even really morning yet?—he could hear his grandmother in the kitchen. She was running water into a pot and clanking dishes in the cabinet. He went out and sat at the table and watched her mixing instant coffee in a mug. "I hope I didn't wake you up," she said.

"What time is it?" Mullen said.

"Four-thirty. I can't sleep a wink past four."

"Christ." He had slept just over an hour.

"Watch it now." His grandmother sat down at the table. "You were a dirty stay-out last night."

"I went to Claude's."

"What a dump. Your grandfather used to go there with Uncle George. Bunch of sad sacks with their cheap beer. Grandpa called it The Cockroach Inn."

"I saw a roach there last night."

"See." She slurped her coffee. "You want some Sanka?"

He shook his head. "I'll go over to the deli and get coffee when it opens."

"Suit yourself. I've got to go to Meat Supreme this morning. What would you like for dinner? Veal cutlets good?"

"Sounds great."

"Fine, I'll get the veal." His grandmother got up and went over to the refrigerator. She took out a Styrofoam container of eggs and a stick of butter. She sliced some butter into her palm, dumping it into a pan on the stove. "You want eggs?"

Mullen put his head down on the table. "Too early," he said.

Mullen woke up and his grandmother was gone. Off to get veal, he guessed. His neck hurt. He didn't know what time it was, but he knew he couldn't have slept for long at the table like that. He went into the living room and checked the clock on the VCR. He was wrong. It was just past eight-thirty.

In the bathroom, he brushed his teeth with his finger and spit blood in the sink.

He changed into his only other clothes and stepped out on the front porch. It was cold. His breath was in front of him.

He walked across the street to Augie's for a coffee.

Augie was just the name that every owner of the store got stuck with. Mullen remembered at least four different Augies, all Chinese, back when he was in the neighborhood. There was an original Augie that his grandparents remembered, an old Italian with hairy hands and an anchor tattoo on his forearm, but he had died in the early Seventies.

The Chinese guy behind the counter now was wearing a Mets cap and a paper apron. He was squat, almost dumpy, with a patches on his neck he'd missed shaving.

Mullen said, "Hey Augie."

The guy nodded.

Mullen went back to where the coffee was and poured himself a large. Black, no sugar.

He sipped it before putting the lid on. He grabbed a *Daily News* on the way up to the counter.

"You new over here?" the guy said, ringing him up.

Mullen put two singles on the counter. "Old. I'm from here. My grandmother lives across the street."

"Where you live now? Somewhere not like this? Going to shit here. The other day, there's a shooting on Twenty-Third Avenue. You believe it?"

"I'm from all over."

"That's the way to be. Don't get tied down. You get a wife like I got a wife, you got a business like I got a business, you're dead."

Mullen nodded and left the store.

The coffee was waking him up, but he didn't know where to go.

He walked back to Claude's, expecting it to be closed. But the door was propped open and Mullen could see Big Connie behind the bar, drinking something from a ricotta container. The floor mats were out front on the sidewalk. Bleach was heavy in the air. Mullen could feel it in his eyes.

Big Connie noticed him and raised her cup. "Kiddo, come on in," she said.

Mullen ducked inside. He pulled up a stool and put his coffee on the bar. "You ever close?" he said.

"Not really," Big Connie said. "Not much difference between being closed and being open anyway. Get you something?"

"Jameson?"

"Good breakfast choice."

Big Connie came over with the bottle in one hand and her drink in the other. Mullen could see that the ricotta container was full of grapefruit juice and he could smell that it was mixed with vodka. 'You want it straight in the coffee?"

"Sure." He took the lid off and she turned the coffee into something better.

He sat there and drank it and watched TV with Big Connie when she flicked it on. When he finished the spiked coffee, she refilled the cup with just Jameson.

***

Around two-thirty, Nancy came in. She was huffing. No one else had been into the bar since he got there. Just Mullen and Big Connie for hours. They'd been watching game shows and soap operas. Mullen was lit.

Nancy said, "I hoped you'd be here." In the daylight she looked like a fat zombie. Her voice was crisp with cigarettes and booze.

"I'm drinking," Mullen said.

"I was just—"

"I'm drinking," he said again.

"Victoria wants to see you."

"Me?"

"She liked having you around. All the guys I've brought home, she's never reacted like this. What you said, it meant a lot to her."

"It was nothing." He paused. "How'd she ask for me? She doesn't talk, does she?"

"She has ways of letting me know things. You don't have to do much. We'll just sit there and watch TV with her."

"Christ," Mullen said, putting his head down on the bar. "My grandmother's making veal for tonight."

"I'll buy you take-out. Whatever you want. Spumoni Gardens."

Walking back to Nancy's house, Mullen felt like it was a trap. He'd had things like this happen to him before. One woman, an office manager at a chiropractor's, was into all sorts of kinky shit. She tied him naked to a chair with bicycle chains and poured honey on his chest. As she licked it off, she pinched his balls with wooden clothespins. Another woman, a secretary from a tire place in Memphis, had locked him in a dark room with five cats for an hour and then came in and attacked him when he was disoriented and sneezing. He wondered how this was going to end. It couldn't be good, not after last night. His mind went back to a scenario that included having Victoria as an audience. Maybe they were some sicko team. Maybe that was the only way for a veg like Victoria to get off.

But when they got back, nothing strange happened. Nancy popped open cans of Bud and they sat on the couch near Victoria, watching TV. Victoria liked basketball, so they watched a rerun of the Knicks playing the Sixers on MSG. She had a Knicks blanket draped over her chest. Mullen had greeted her with a pat on the head and every once in a while she strained her head in his direction, her eyes floating up, and purred.

Nancy said, "I'm her only friend now. The Jamaican who stayed with her on weekdays while I was at work had to go home."

"Too bad," Mullen said.

"She likes you."

Mullen felt like he was in a horror movie. Like any second he'd find out that he was food for Victoria. He pictured Nancy coming after him with a cleaver, saying, "She needs a sacrifice! She needs a sacrifice!"

He was starting to feel uncomfortable.

"She really likes you," Nancy said again.

Mullen stared at Victoria. Her throat fluttered. The mask seemed to heave. Her face was crumpled, desperate. He stood up and went over to her and patted her on the head roughly, the way you would a third grade boy or a randy dog. His skin came away covered in ointment. "I like her, too," Mullen said.

Victoria made a clicking sound in the back of her throat.

"She's so happy," Nancy said.

Mullen backed away.

Nancy stood up. "I've got an idea. Wait there. Talk to her."

She disappeared into the bedroom, and Mullen heard her throw open the closet door. Mullen looked down at Victoria. "That's a girl," he said. "Easy now."

Nancy came back out with a fedora in her palm. It looked like the kind they sold on Eighty-Sixth Street, a knock-off, with a feather scotch-taped to the side. She plopped it on Victoria's head.

In her hospital gown, Knicks blanket, and cheapo fedora, Victoria looked like a fucked dress-up doll.

"I was in *Guys and Dolls* in high school," Nancy said. "I played Nathan Detroit. Victoria always liked when I came home from rehearsals and put my hat on her. She'd dance around. She used to love to dance."

Tears lipped Victoria's eyes. He couldn't imagine having everything trapped on the inside like that, not being able to mouth a word or move a hand. It'd be one thing just to be a crip parked in front of the TV all day, but this was a different kind of prison.

Nancy started to move Victoria's chair around in a circle, miming dance, and the IV tubes jiggled and webbed around them. She hummed, unable to remember words to any of the songs. Mullen swelled with sadness. He remembered feeling like this one other time at a shelter in Kansas City when an old black guy with a speckled beard shit himself and got hosed down by a doughy attendant in front of all the other residents.

Mullen put his elbow up on the handle of Victoria's chair and stopped Nancy from spinning her. "Not sure she likes it," he said.

"Sure she does," Nancy said.

"I don't know." Mullen untangled two tubes over Victoria's shoulder and kneeled next to her.

Nancy huffed. "You're Prince Charming all of a sudden?"

"She just . . ."

"Come to the bedroom with me. I want to show you something."

"What about Victoria?"

"She'll be here."

The something Nancy wanted to show him looked like a saddle with a dildo protruding from the top. A thick black wire ran from the side to a boxy remote with a red knob.

"It's called a Sybian," she said.

The device plugged into the wall. She twisted the red knob and the dildo started buzzing. She slipped out of her sweatpants. No underwear. She licked her hand. Ran it between her legs. Mounted the machine. Writhing, she put her hands up in her hair.

Mullen watched her lazy eye. Sullen, glassy, it seemed to just float there as her body rumbled.

"Come over here," she said, her voice thrumming.

He stood in front of her and she unbuckled his pants and pushed them down and took him in her mouth. He was half-hard. Her mouth felt rubbery. He could feel her teeth on him. The buzz of the machine made it difficult to focus. Victoria on the other side of the wall, in her fedora and Knicks blanket, made it difficult to focus. Nancy was moaning on him, trying to make him stiffer.

Mullen closed his eyes. He tried to picture just the mouth on him. Not the teeth in the mouth. Not the tongue. Not the hideous face around the mouth. But it wasn't enough. He softened to a dangle and backed away from Nancy.

"What's wrong?" she said.

"It's too much," he said.

Nancy bucked on the Sybian. "Your loss," she said.

He watched her. Hands under her shirt. Horrible. He shuffled out to Victoria, his pants around his knees. He stood next to her. "Christ," he said. "You've got it rough, huh?"

Her face frosted over.

He moved in front of her and he felt her eyes hone in on his pecker. There was no way to be sure with eyes like that, but they seemed to be tilting in the general direction of his crotch. He wondered if she'd ever seen a pecker. Probably not. Fifteen when she got hit by that bus.

He flipped his pecker with two fingers and tried to force wood. It wouldn't take. "No luck today," he said and then paused. "You ever seen a wang? I'd hate for this to be your first. It's puny." And it was. It wasn't well-maintained either. Rarely scrubbed clean. Knobby with warts. "But, generally speaking, peckers are nothing to write home about. They just remind me of big bags of donated clothes sitting outside the Knights of Columbus."

Victoria seemed to be taking in what he was saying. It was the most he'd spoken in a long time.

"I can really talk to you," he said, pulling up his pants. "I'm gonna leave now, but I'll come back to visit. I'll bring pignoli cookies."

Mullen went down the water and smoked a cigarette he'd bummed from a car service guy near Wendy's on the way.

When he was a kid, he'd come here and sneak cigs with a Russian named Vlad. They'd talk and he wouldn't understand a word that Vlad was saying. He'd met Vlad in the Victory Memorial ER, where he did his service as a junior at Our Lady of the Narrows. Vlad was a janitor with tattoos. Mullen liked him more than the guinea nurses who skeeved the wild-eyed Asians that filled the ER.

Mullen had left Nancy on the Sybian and Victoria in front of the TV and here he was thinking about a goddamn nobody Russian that probably died the way Russians always died. In the cold. He thought of the clicking sound Victoria had made with her throat. It seemed so genuine.

He flicked his cigarette into the bay and walked the few blocks back to Claude's. The TV was showing

Cheers. Big Connie was slumped behind the bar with a crossword puzzle.

Mullen had missed his grandmother's veal. He was feeling booze-wobbly. When he got home, he'd collect his hidden dough and rest a little. In the morning, he'd wait for his grandmother to go to the store and then he'd paperclip a wad of twenties to her morning scratch-off tickets and leave for the next place before she got back.

HERE COME THE BELLS

I.

By the time I got to Coney Island, I'd started to worry that Uncle Harry wouldn't be happy to see me. I hadn't had much time to let him know I was coming. I'd tried calling, but the phone just rang and rang. I'd sent a postcard a few days before, telling him about what had happened in Texas and that I had nowhere else to go and when I should be getting to town. I really had no other options. I'd thought about going to visit Ricky Marsh in Philly, but was I just gonna shack up on his floor for the rest of my life? He had a sorority slick wife.

Uncle Harry owned a hotel in Coney Island called The Terminal, and that's all I was returning to. It was more like a rooming house, but even that was being too kind. Red Pete, a pimp, ran a few girls out of the five or six rooms on the third floor. The second floor was occupied by drunks and junkies who needed a flop. My uncle always cut them a break because he was a drunk and he used to be a junkie. The ground floor was for permanent residents: Uncle Harry, Holdout, Belly

Talbot, and Jimmy Gimmick's ex-wife Whistler. As far as I knew, not much had changed since I'd spent all my time there as a kid.

When I got off the train, I noticed how different the station was. They'd reconstructed it. I didn't know the names for the things they'd done, but it looked clean and new and it felt empty. I stepped outside and saw that other things had changed but not much. They'd put in a minor league baseball stadium, and they'd cleaned up the Boardwalk some. I walked around with my hands in my pockets and my backpack slung over my shoulder. I didn't have much with me, just some clothes, a couple of paperbacks, my electric razor, and tweezers because my eyebrows connected if I didn't pluck them every month.

Uncle Harry's hotel was crumbling. Even worse than I remembered. The sign was unhinged, three of the letters caved in. The brick was salt-worn and splatted with pigeon shit. Half of the windows were boarded. The glass on the front door was shattered and it'd been duct-taped with heavy plastic that bubbled in the wind. A stool right outside the front door was overturned. The buzzer was tagged over with green spray paint.

I buzzed. Nothing. I buzzed again. Still nothing. I wasn't even sure the buzzer was working. I heard a little hiccup when I pushed the button but there should've been a steady gurgle. I tried the door. Locked. I knocked with my fist. I was cold. When you live in Texas for ten years and come back to New York, the cold gets right down to your bones. It was about thirty, icy and a little windy, but it felt like a negative thousand to me. My coat wasn't that heavy. My socks were sweaty.

I stood there for fifteen minutes and then figured I'd have to find another way in. An alley around back led to a door that Uncle Harry sometimes propped open. He'd smoke out there with Holdout when they needed a break from Whistler or when the weather was nice enough to turn over a milk crate and play Hearts.

Uncle Harry was in the alley when I got there. He was wearing a bathrobe and looking up at a seagull. He'd lost most of his hair and a few front teeth. He had a lit cigarette in each hand and he wasn't smoking either one. He was barefoot. His nose looked like it'd been trampled.

"Uncle Harry," I said.

He looked at me and tried to focus. "Christ. Foley."

"You get my postcard?"

"Sure I did. It's mighty good to see you, boy."

I went over and hugged him. He smelled like vinegar. His arms were bristly like a shoebrush.

"Don't mind the smell," he said. "Been putting vinegar on my gums."

"I was worried you didn't get my card."

"Chased out of Texas. You'll have to tell me all about it."

"It's okay if I stay?"

"Okay?" He came over and hugged me again. "Of course, boy. You can live here until you croak if you want. Got a room all ready for you. First floor, so it's a little fancier. If Magnuson ever comes around with a girl, you'll have to give it up for a few hours, but that's the only hitch." He dropped both cigarettes and stomped them out.

"Who's Magnuson?"

"Christ, you've been gone a long time. Magnuson's a big deal. Magnuson's kind of like the mayor."

"Does he come here a lot?" I said.

"He's got two wives and about ten goomars. He comes here when he wants one of Red Pete's girls. Mostly Big Fay."

"How've you been?"

Uncle Harry opened his mouth. "These goddamn gums." He was talking with his mouth open and it was hard to understand him. "They give me a lot of heartache."

"I'm sure."

He closed his mouth. "You look good. Football star."

"I just played two years in high school."

"Still. Who'd a thought?"

"You heard from my mother?"

"Guatemala. Christ. Your mother's whacked out. Since your old man kicked, she's been whacked out. He was around, he would've been against Texas."

My father died when I was three. I had no real memories of him. One or two cloudy pictures. Him standing in my doorway one night as my mother put me to bed. His beard, his sunken eyes. Uncle Harry was my father's best friend, that's how he became my uncle. They went to Boody together. My father died of heart failure. At least that's what I'd always been told. He and Uncle Harry had been tied up with some shady people. I'd heard that later around The Terminal. Guys like Chick Nelson and Tony D'Abruzzo. I'd always wondered if maybe he'd been gunned down. I also always wondered what the difference between heart failure and a heart attack was. Heart failure sounded so much worse, like his heart had just given up. At least a heart attack sounded like there'd been a battle, an effort. If you're going to make something up, why not make up heart attack? My old man. He was like the saints in the windows at church. Just a thing they talked about. *Your old man used to be the king of craps in the alley. Your old man climbed the Parachute Jump. Your old man lost his cherry on the Wonder Wheel. Your old man drag-raced on Eighty-Sixth Street. Your old man smoked Luckies. He made his own wine. He was a prince.*

"Forget about your mother," Uncle Harry said. "I told your old man don't marry a mick. Can't cook. Teeth rotten by thirty. Prone to being a goddamn nutjob. Come in, let me get you settled."

I followed Uncle Harry inside. The hall was a dark twist of shadows and bleach smells. The walls were rotten. I saw shapes of faces in the wood. Uncle Harry once told me he and my father had insulated the walls with Schaefer's cans. "Hasn't changed," I said.

"I get these kids from downtown now," Uncle Harry said. "Come over and rent rooms for a few hours just to drink and feel like they're slumming it. I get writers. Show up with cellphones their mothers are paying for. I get guys in trucker caps, they want to bag a hooker but they don't have the guts. They spend an hour in the goddamn room and then get right back on the train. I'm like one of those old dive bars that the shitheads find."

A cramped booth served as the front desk. A strongbox was hidden under the floorboards. Uncle Harry only took cash. He had ledgers, but I'm not sure he kept track of anything.

He said, "You want a beer?"

"Sure," I said.

We went into the bathroom and he wrestled the lid off the toilet tank. He had beers sunk in the filmy water. He took out two cans and tossed one to me. I thumbed open the tab and drank.

"It's good to see you, boy," Uncle Harry said.

"I don't know what I'll do," I said. "Job-wise."

"We'll get you figured out. You relax now. Finish that and then get some rest."

Uncle Harry showed me into a room at the end of the hall and then left me alone. Magnuson's fuckpad. Whoever Magnuson was. Looked like a hideout where money would be split up. I'd never been in there before. At one point, I think, it had been Belly Talbot's room. I wondered if Belly Talbot was gone or dead. The lampshade was the color of burnt butter and the dull light made you feel like you were inside a jellyfish. A cracked mirror hung on one wall. The bed was square and flat, a thin blanket over it sprinkled with ceiling shavings, the pillows knobby. A radiator in the corner chuckled and hissed. The wood floor was saggy, wet-looking in spots. I sat down on the bed and took off my shoes. I put my pack in my lap. It smelled like Texas.

Uncle Harry opened the door and stuck his head back in. "You want I should ask Red Pete to send a girl down? On me."

"No," I said. "Thanks. I'm beat." And I was. I hadn't slept well—or at all, really—on the bus.

Uncle Harry ducked out. I closed my eyes.

* * *

I woke up I didn't know how much later to Uncle Harry shaking my shoulder. My eyes sputtered open. "I need to get you out of here," Uncle Harry said.

"What?" I said.

"Magnuson's coming."

"Already?"

"Magnuson comes when Magnuson comes."

Uncle Harry hustled me and my pack upstairs to room 306. The window was broken and taped over with flimsy plastic. I could feel the cold being piped in. The bed was on the floor, mud-crusted bricks scattered around it. I didn't ask about the bricks. The air smelled of piss and aftershave. "Listen, I'm sorry," Uncle Harry said. "Just rotten luck Magnuson's coming tonight. I sprayed the room for bugs yesterday. There's nothing to worry about."

I sat on the bed, my pack in my lap. I wasn't tired anymore. What I did sometimes when I couldn't sleep was write postcards in my head to all the people I'd ever known. I wrote to my old man even though he was dead, to my mother in Guatemala, to my aunt in Austin, to Uncle Harry, to Rosalia, who was my girlfriend from before I left Brooklyn, and to plenty of others. I imagined myself sitting down at a table with a blue pen. I'm not sure where the table was. I imagined sitting there with a stack of cards and I saw it like in a movie: the pen moving, words forming. My handwriting in my imagination was much better than it was in real life. I heard the words in voiceover, too. That also felt like a movie. I didn't recognize the voice reading them. It was kind of sad and flat. The postcards were never long. Just how are you and do you remember the time and I'm okay kind of stuff. Now I was writing one to my mother, saying I was back in the old neighborhood and what was Guatemala like and did she have a job yet.

My eyes were closed. I guessed I wouldn't sleep all night. I wrote more postcards and then I thought about going outside. I wondered if Roy-Roy's was open for a falafel or if it was even still around. I'd go there all the time with my mom when I was a kid. She liked anything that wasn't Italian. Middle Eastern. Vietnamese. Indian. Anything that felt exotic. Roy-Roy's was just okay falafels and fries, but it was a place that felt familiar. I doubted anything was open. I didn't even know what time it was. It had to be the middle of the night. I didn't know if Magnuson had arrived or how long he would be around.

I got up and went out into the hallway. It was warmer. I sat down near a heat pipe. I could hear the heat coming up in the pipe and that was one of my least favorite sounds. I saw a roach on the floor at the end of the hall. It was the size of a mouse. I couldn't sleep in the hall.

I went back downstairs and poked around, thinking maybe I'd find a short dog of wine Uncle Harry or Holdout had stashed somewhere. One of the lights in the hallway was flickering. I could still hear the heat coming up. On top of that, I heard fucking noises from behind one of the doors. I couldn't tell which door, and they weren't normal fucking noises. The woman wasn't moaning, wasn't saying anything that you say during sex. What she was doing was kind of a prolonged grunt. It sounded like she was passing a kidney stone. And the guy, he was just whooping. Over and over. Whoop, whoop, whoop.

The noises stopped. A door at the end of the hallway opened and light spilled out onto the cement-colored rug. A guy wearing nothing stepped out into the hallway. He was the one that had been whooping. His dick was still half-hard, a loose-fitting neon green condom drooping off. He had hair on his chest and shoulders and he was wearing fuzzy black slippers. He was maybe two thirty and six-two. He saw me and started to walk in my direction. "You out here listening?" he said.

"No, sir," I said. "Just looking for my uncle."

"Your uncle?"

"Uncle Harry."

"You're Harry's nephew?"

"Foley." He was close to me now, and I stuck out my hand to shake.

"You don't want to shake with me right now," he said. "I was just elbow deep in Big Fay. Harry's talked about you."

"You're Mr. Magnuson?"

"Christ, you're polite. That's me." He looked like a Ray Liotta knockoff. He had twinkly blue eyes, a gritty complexion, and small scars on his cheeks and arms.

"I heard you're like the mayor."

He smiled and I saw a mouthful of caps. "The mayor, that's good. I am like the mayor."

"I'm going to go back upstairs," I said.

"You need work?"

"What?"

"You want to work for me? I'm looking for a guy I could trust. And if you're Uncle Harry's nephew."

"I—maybe."

"Think about it. I'm on Mermaid. Got an office in the back of Jackie Kiddo's garage. You know the place?"

"I think so."

"Good meeting you, kid."

II.

The next day at Jackie Kiddo's garage Magnuson was straight with me. He said this is what I need you to do and if you don't like the sound of it, bail now. He told me I'd be going after guys who owed. He told me I might have to do some stuff to get the dough. Snap a bone. Clip off a toe. Make them understand what was on the line. He said if it came to that, do what needed to be done and then give them one day to make good.

I never figured on getting into strongarm work, but sometimes you're painted into a corner and the worst options are the best options.

Magnuson stuffed some cash in my pocket and said, "You start now." He wrote down an address on Bay Parkway and Cropsey. Said the guy, Georgie, owed BIG. He gave me a car, an old Dodge beater with a rusty body that pulsed.

Rosalia used to live not far from where this guy Georgie was. The whole way over I was thinking about her. What I wasn't thinking about was how I'd approach this guy. I didn't know what to do if he wasn't home. I was guessing Magnuson would want me to wait for him. I was wondering if I could get into a situation where I'd just have to sit and wait all day.

I parked at a hydrant. His apartment was on the third floor of a three-family house. I just went up and knocked on his door.

A guy answered, dark-complected and skinny, wearing a Knicks jersey, basketball shorts, and sneakers with no laces. "Yeah?" he said.

"You Georgie?" I said.

"Fuck are you?"

I popped him in the nose and he fell back into the house. I didn't want to give him the chance to get ready. I'd been in a few scrapes, and I could throw a punch.

He flopped around and held his face. Blood was pouring out of his nose. His jersey was already covered.

"Magnuson wants what you owe him," I said.

"I'm not late."

"I don't know about late."

"He said have it to him by the fifth. Today's the third. I got two days."

"I don't know about two days."

"Go see him and ask."

"I'm not leaving without the money."

"Christ," he said. "You gotta know how to run a business. This is no way to do it. He said the fifth. Call him. Just do me a favor."

Maybe he was telling the truth. But maybe he was just trying to get me out of there or get me with my back to him while I called Magnuson's office. "Consider today the fifth," I said.

"Christ. Let me go in the bedroom and see what I got."

I followed him to the bedroom, not trusting him enough to leave him alone, and watched as he started to go through drawers. He was looking everywhere, making a show of it. "I've got something here somewhere," he said.

The next thing I knew he dashed for the window, threw it open, and climbed out onto the fire escape. The fire escape went down to the lower level roof and then there was another ladder to the ground. He was so fast, it looked like he'd practiced his getaway. I was just sticking a foot out the window and he'd already hit the ground in the yard and taken off toward Eighty-Sixth Street.

I figured there was no use running after him, so I took my time climbing down and then went back to the car. I wasn't nervous. I figured I'd find him. I figured he was headed for the train, and I knew I could beat him there.

The train was exactly where he was going. I parked on the corner of Bay Parkway and Eighty-Sixth Street and waited. It didn't take long for him to show. He couldn't run that well with no laces and people were looking at him with the blood all over his shirt.

I got out of the car, and I clotheslined him off his feet. He came out of his shoes and groaned. I dragged him over to the car. Threw him in the back seat. "My shoes," he said. "They're still out there."

"Forget your shoes." I dug around in the glovebox. I was hoping there was something I could use to scare Georgie. I found a stack of old Esso maps and the car's papers, that was it. I turned around and looked at him.

He was totally wiped out. I said, "We're going back to your place and we're gonna get whatever money you have. The rest you need to have by this time tomorrow."

Georgie nodded.

I wasn't thinking about what if he ran off before paying the rest. I was just doing what I was told.

Georgie owed twelve large. Turned out he had three grand hidden in a blender box under his kitchen sink. He gave me the money without any hassle. He even started trying to pal around with me. I told him I'd be back the next day and he started crying. "I'm not sure I can get the money," he said.

"You have to," I said.

"I'll try," he said. "I'll try to borrow from my mom. She won't be happy. She's saving up for a flatscreen TV."

I didn't saying anything. I left. I put the money in the glovebox of the Dodge and drove away.

Rosalia's house was on Bay Thirty-Eighth Street between Bath and Cropsey. I parked out front and turned the car off and just sat there for a while. I doubted she still lived at home.

The house looked pretty much the same. Washed-out red brick, the trim on the windows painted white. Grapevines on crumbling trellises in the front yard. Withered tomato plants on sticks. Overturned buckets painted red. Concrete lions painted red. A statue of Saint Rosalia in the garden that leaned right. Saint Rosalia wore a brown gown and held a skull on a book in one hand, a cross in the other. A rosary dangled from her waist. She was wearing a crown of red roses. Her nose was chipped. Rosalia told me that her family used to have a statue of the Virgin Mary in the front yard like so many other families in the neighborhood, but that her dad took it inside on the day she was born and put out the statue of Saint Rosalia. The Mary statue went on the windowsill of her mother's bedroom (her dad had his own room on the third floor and he had a picture of Sophia Loren in his closet). Rosalia's mom, who everyone called Mama Fanny, turned Mary facing out to the yard when she was praying for nice weather.

Saint Rosalia was the patron saint of Palermo, which is where Rosalia's dad was from. I didn't even know his first name. I'd never called him anything other than Mr. Campagna. I didn't know that much about him. I knew he'd grown up in Palermo and left for New York when he was seventeen. I knew he met Mama Fanny two weeks after arriving, and I knew she was sixteen when they got married. I knew about the Sophia Loren picture. I knew he owned a pork store in Dyker Heights. I knew he made his own wine in the basement and that he liked eating *soppressata* off a paring knife.

I took the money with me and got out of the car. I'd been in Rosalia's room almost every day for two years before I left for Texas. We kissed on her bed and in her closet. I pulled her sweater off over her head a thousand times and touched her tits through her bra. We locked the door and turned the music so loud it rattled the walls. Mama Fanny would always come up and bang on the door and tell us to unlock it and lower the music. We never fucked because we were both scared of her getting pregnant, but she blew me a bunch and I fingered her. She wasn't good at blowing me when she started—she scraped me with her teeth and had no rhythm—but she got way better as time went on. It was hard to even go that far with her mother hawking over us, but we got it done—sometimes in the closet, sometimes in the basement, sometimes right there in the bed with a mess of blankets over us. Her room always smelled like sandalwood. And the sandalwood would mix with the smell of the gravy her mom was cooking—the basil, the garlic browned in olive oil. It was the greatest smell I'd ever known. What I wanted just at that moment was to be fifteen again and for Rosalia to be fifteen again and for us to be kissing in her closet with that smell in the air.

I pressed the bell and waited. I was nervous. If Rosalia was there, I wasn't sure I'd know how to talk to her. We were kids last time we'd seen each other and now we were in our late twenties. Plus I was wearing ratty old clothes, and I didn't know what I smelled like. I hoped decent. I hadn't showered in a few days but Uncle Harry had given me deodorant and a toothbrush.

The door opened and there was Mama Fanny. She seemed shorter and fatter and balder. She was wearing a housedress stained with gravy, a purple dishrag slung over her shoulder. She was pale and sweaty. The warmth of the house hit me full in the face. I could smell gravy cooking. But I also smelled wet boxes and dust and a bottled-up sourness. "You one of them Watchtower people?" she said.

"Mama Fanny, I'm—"

"How do you know me?"

"I'm Foley. From high school. I used to go with Rosalia."

She looked me up and down. "Foley?" she said. "With the trench coat and the long hair?"

"That's me."

"Foley who moved to Texas?"

"I'm back. I'm staying in Coney Island with my uncle."

She looked sad suddenly. Tears rimmed her eyes.

"I'm sorry," I said. "If it's a bad time, I can come back. I didn't know if Rosalia still lived here or what. I just thought I'd see if she was here, say hello."

"She's still here," Mama Fanny said. "Come in."

She took me inside. She wiped her eyes with the backs of her hands. "You sure now is okay?" I said.

"It doesn't matter when. I'm glad you came by."

The living room was the same. Green shag rug. Plastic on the couches. A painting of the Mediterranean on the wall. A framed picture of Jesus on top of the old box TV. She told me to sit down on the couch. I did. She asked if I wanted anything to drink. Coffee. Diet Coke. I said I'd love a coffee. She disappeared into the kitchen and came back with a demitasse cup full to the brim on a saucer. "Sugar?" she said. "Milk?"

"No," I said, "that's okay."

She sat down on a chair across from me and put the purple dishrag in her lap.

I sipped my coffee. "So, where's Rosalia?" I said.

"She's in her room."

"Upstairs? Can I go up?"

"Her room's downstairs now. That room right off the kitchen. We had to move her down here."

"She's not well?"

Mama Fanny put her hands on her knees. "She started in college at Kingsborough. Normal kid. She was a little upset after you moved, but she stopped with the mascara and the wearing all black and started volunteering at St. Mary's. Then she got a job in Dr. Zucco's office on Eighty-Third Street. When she was nineteen going on twenty, a week before her birthday, she had, like, this stroke. The doctors said it was probably just something that had been in her all along. I don't know. She couldn't walk. Couldn't talk. It left her mind off."

I looked down at the rug. I tried to picture Rosalia as a vegetable. "How's she now?" I said.

"Not much better. She can't talk. She can make sounds. Her sister comes over to visit every week. Mr. Campagna never really got over it. I do what needs to be done."

"I'm so sorry." I stood up. "I should just go."

"Don't. She never gets visitors other than her sister. The girls from the office used to come by, but they stopped. She never really had a boyfriend after you."

"She never had a boyfriend after me?"

"A couple of guys she saw, but no one she liked."

I wondered if she'd ever blown another guy. "It's okay if I visit her?" I said.

Mama Fanny nodded. "I wish you would."

She led me through the kitchen, where I deposited my coffee cup in the deep basin of the sink and looked longingly at the gravy simmering on the stove, into Rosalia's room. Rosalia was tucked under tight sheets, her eyes closed, her face powdery, her hair parted dramatically. She looked so much older and thin like she'd been on hunger strike. She gulped constantly, throaty swallows that seemed to rattle her chest. Her upper lip had been shaved. So had her arms. She wore one of Mama Fanny's too-big housedresses, green ivy and red roses wired around the fabric in twisty patterns. Her feet, sticking out from under the blankets, were bare and they'd been moisturized to a shine. I'd expected tubes and IV bags and wires. Machines. The kind that keep people breathing. It wasn't like that.

"She eats some," Mama Fanny said. "Applesauce is her favorite. Sometimes we liquefy pasta and gravy. Mostly, it's pureed sweet potatoes. Soft things. Baby food."

"She eats baby food?" I said.

Mama Fanny nodded and sat on the edge of the bed, putting her hand on Rosalia's foot. "Terrible, isn't it? So young and she's like an old woman on her deathbed. But you can't question God. He has his reasons, I'm sure."

"You think God has reasons for this?"

"Sure. Absolutely. Nothing happens that God doesn't want to happen."

"I should go," I said. "She's sleeping."

"It's okay. Don't."

"I should." I backed out of the room into the kitchen.

Mama Fanny followed me. "Come back. When she's awake. Come back and visit. Please."

"I will. I promise."

Mama Fanny started crying again. "She'll be so happy to see you."

"How are you for money? There must be bills."

"They just pile up. We just got one for five thousand, you believe that? Some test."

I took the cash Magnuson stuffed in my pocket—it was a hundred bucks—and put it on the kitchen table. Then I peeled a few bills off the stack I'd gotten from Georgie and put that on the table. "I hope this helps."

"That's so kind of you, Foley." She threw herself at me and wrapped her arms around my back and sobbed into my chest.

"I'll be back when I can," I said. "I'll bring money when I can."

III.

"I don't like it, you working for Magnuson," Uncle Harry said.

"I know," I said.

"He's a dangerous guy."

"He's pretty straightforward."

"Straightforward, my ass."

We were in Uncle Harry's room. He was sitting on the edge of the bed, clipping his toenails. I was squatting on the floor, trying not to feel cold. I'd told him about Magnuson and about going after Georgie. I'd also told him about Rosalia. He'd shaken his head at all of it.

"Trouble, boy," he said now. "You're asking for it."

I was due at Magnuson's in two hours. It was a couple of days after I'd started working for him, and I'd already been back to settle up with Georgie. I'd half-expected him to be gone, missing, when I showed up for the rest of the dough, but he was home and he had banded stacks of bills in a duffel bag. I wasn't yet sure how I was going to account for the money I'd given Mama Fanny, but I didn't care. As soon as I saw the pile, I knew I'd skim a few hundred more for Rosalia. If what Georgie handed over was a grand short I figured it'd be easy to pin on him. It was his word against mine. I'd stopped and visited with Rosalia again, leaving a few hundred in an envelope on the kitchen table. She was asleep, and I just sat there and looked at her. Mama Fanny talked about Mr. Campagna maybe coming downstairs, but he never did. I didn't stay long. I went and dropped the rest of the money with Magnuson at Jackie Kiddo's. "Good," he'd said. He didn't count it or even open the bag. He just wrote something in a marble notebook and told me to come back the next day, which I did. I had to collect a few grand from a bearded doctor in Bay Ridge on that run, which was easy. "It's not trouble," I said to Uncle Harry. "I'm just trying to help."

When I showed up at Jackie Kiddo's that afternoon, I was directed to the roof by Peggy Sorensen, one of Magnuson's goomars. I went up a wooden staircase. I wasn't thinking about it being the roof. I wasn't thinking about being dangled for thieving. Magnuson was up there, waving a black flag, guiding a kit of pigeons in a circle overhead. He was moving in front of a well-constructed coop with tar paper laid out to catch all the pigeon shit. The landing board was open. "Kid," he said. "Welcome. Have a seat." He pointed to a turned-over milk crate.

I sat down and looked up at the pigeons. They were beautiful in their motions, like a swirl of gray paint against the blue sky. "Do you race them?" I said.

"I sure do," he said. "They're fucking champs. Thoroughbreds of the air."

"I always wanted to be into pigeons."

"My pigeons aren't why you're here. You've taken some money. I think I understand why. Rosalia."

I said nothing.

"I do my research. Ultimately, I can't fault you. It makes me like you, you wanting to take care of this poor broad. That said, you're stealing. I'd prefer not to throw you off the roof, so here's what we're gonna do: You're gonna fight for me. You're gonna earn the dough you took. And you'll keep earning dough and you can give that to Rosalia's family."

"Fight for you?"

"In the smokers. Boxing. You played football, right? I know you can punch." He put down the flag and came over to me. He pinched my cheek. "Sounds good, right? Fucking *Raging Bull*."

"I used to box a little in the gym," I said.

"There you go. First fight's tomorrow . . ." The pigeons flooded into the coop, and I lost Magnuson's voice in the engine sound of their wings. They finally settled down. They weren't like the ratty pigeons on the streets. They were smooth and clean. I wanted to hold one in my hands.

"Tomorrow?" I said. "I need to train."

"We're not raising you up to be a contender, kid. You get in there, you punch, you get hit. Simple. And you're still doing the other thing. You're into me big. I've got you for life. You're one of my pigeons." He laughed from the gut, big and sweaty.

I left the roof, thankful in retrospect for not having been dangled, for not having had a finger lopped off, for not having a pigeon stuffed down my throat. I went back to Uncle Harry's and put on sweats and went for a run on the Boardwalk. I shadow-boxed on the beach. It wasn't pretty. I was slow. I felt it in my lungs. I wasn't in bad shape, but I certainly wasn't in good shape. Even if I got a few good jabs in or took punches like a pro, I'd be surprised if I had the stamina to go more than a round. But maybe that was what Magnuson wanted. His expectations were low. He just needed a body, one that people wouldn't automatically laugh off, and I wasn't soft.

When I told Uncle Harry about it in the alley, he just pressed his thumbs against his gums and let out a spitty wheeze. "See how fast," he said.

"How fast what?" I said.

"How fast you get caught up in it. Next thing you know, five years have passed and then ten and then you're dead because you pissed Magnuson off. Get on a bus. Don't go to Texas. Don't go find your mother in Guatemala. Go somewhere new. Start over. I'll pay Magnuson back. He'll forget."

"I want to help Rosalia."

"You can't stick it in a vegetable. Forget her, boy. She's gone."

"Christ, Unc."

Uncle Harry shrugged. "I'm trying to help you here."

I didn't sleep well that night. I wrote postcards in my head. I wrote one to Rosalia. I said I was sorry I didn't keep in touch with her all those years ago. I said I was sorry that I just stopped being her boyfriend because of Texas. I kept seeing her face in that bed where she stayed, saint-thin and shivery. I told her that I was sorry that no amount of sorry was going to change anything for her. I told her I would get her family any money I could. I signed the postcard as her boyfriend because I felt like her boyfriend again even though she wasn't much more than a ghost.

The smoker was in a warehouse on Neptune Avenue. About a hundred folding chairs circled a ring. Smoke from cigars clouded the ceiling. There wasn't a dressing room. Magnuson showed me to a corner of the warehouse and sat me on a stool and had Jackie Kiddo tape my hands. I wasn't wearing trunks. I was wearing sweatpants cut above the knee. Jackie took off my shirt and oiled my chest. None of us talked. I looked around. I wanted a glimpse of the other fighter. I wondered if he was in a corner too, being greased and taped. They stood me up, and Magnuson jabbed at my belly. I jerked back. He shook his head.

"Don't forget to protect yourself," Jackie Kiddo said. He slipped black gloves on me. They were too big. My hands were swimming in them. He shoved a mouthpiece in my mouth as if he were giving a dog medicine.

"This guy went over and fucked your vegetable girlfriend," Magnuson said. "He opened her up with some Vaseline and just had at her. You're gonna let him get away with it?"

Music blazed from speakers that surrounded the ring. Magnuson pushed me toward the action. I entered through the ropes, which were lower to the ground than they should've been. I was alone in the ring for a minute, spinning around, and then I found my way to a corner where Jackie Kiddo plopped down a stool and made me sit.

The other guy entered. He wasn't what I expected. He wasn't tall, maybe five-six, but he had about forty pounds on me and no tattoos and was pale as milk with a twist of red hair screwed onto his head. "There's the guy that fucked Rosalia," Magnuson whispered in my ear through the ropes.

A ref came into the ring but he wasn't dressed like a ref. He wore a red tracksuit, the zipper open on a white V-neck. The folding chairs filled in with fat faces chomping on cigars, eating sausage-and-pepper sandwiches wrapped in tinfoil. I knew that there were smokers that were legitimate, sanctioned, whatever, but I knew this wasn't one of them. It was just some underground thing, slopped together as a way to gamble. Put two chumps in the ring and let them have at each other, see who comes out on top. The redhead was no more of a boxer than I was. He looked like he'd given up the priesthood. He looked like he was trying to pay off student loans. I imagined that the mobsters in the crowd bet based on looks. With forty pounds on me, the redhead looked more powerful, more capable of damage. I wondered about the bets being made. No doubt they had me as an underdog. Did they have me going down in the first?

And how long would they let it go?

The fight started with a bell, and the redhead plodded around me. He probably had a nastiness in him but right then he looked gentle, like he helped his grandmother go shopping for groceries. I pictured him on top of Rosalia and started swinging.

His punches, when he finally started hitting back, slid off of me. I didn't feel like I was moving. I heard him saying bad things to Rosalia in my head.

I drilled him in the face with a hard right, and his nose opened up. The blood curtained over his mouth and chin. It arced down and painted his chest with a bolt of red. He looked like something lost and helpless. I still heard him talking to Rosalia in my head. I wasn't sorry. I wanted to punch into the blood and paleness.

I went back to the face with my right. He spun around to try to slip my punches. I brought a left up from underneath and hit him in the chest where he'd been marked with blood.

He fell to the canvas.

I heard sounds through the smoke. Wheezes of disappointment.

Jackie Kiddo found me in the center of the ring and put my arms up. "Fuck, kid," he said. "You're a monster."

On the ride back to Jackie's garage, Magnuson said, "That was pleasant, kid. I knew you'd take that bum."

"I'm no boxer," I said. "I'm just lucky he was less of one."

"'Lucky,' shit. You got a golden swing. And these smokers are full of half-assed fighters. You're not gonna see Tyson in there. Even the *tizzuns* we bring in are soft."

I tongued the back of my teeth.

"You're working off your debt," Magnuson said. "That's good." He took a fold of bills out of his jacket pocket and thumbed off two fifties. "Here's a hundred for your poor little vegetable. She's your muse, I appreciate that."

I pocketed the money.

"This afternoon, you're putting on your other hat. There's this Russian, Vlad, he owes. He hangs on the Boardwalk. Go collect. No skimming this time, okay? After that, you go can go see Rosalia."

I looked out the window. We were passing a salvage yard.

"And remember," Magnuson said. "You cross me, I drown your vegetable girlfriend like a kitten."

Vlad was easy to find. He had a kid with him. Blond, maybe eight or nine. I didn't know if the kid was his or not, but I didn't want him to be there if I had to hurt the poor old fucker. I tried to shoo the kid away. Tried to give him a couple of bucks for a hot dog. But he didn't move, and he didn't speak. They both just sat there, looking sad and Russian. Vlad had the air of a degenerate gambler. His clothes smelled of smoke from backroom card games. "You've gotta settle with Magnuson," I said.

He just nodded.

"You understand me, right?"

He nodded again.

"I can't leave . . ."

He stood up and pointed out at the water. "Maybe I'll just drown myself," he said.

"Don't talk like that in front of the kid," I said.

"You're right. My son doesn't deserve this." He kicked into a run and headed for the shoreline.

I gave the kid a look, like *Jesus Christ, really?* The kid's eyes showed nothing. He was stone. It was like he was used to watching his old man bolt for the shoreline. Vlad was probably the kind of guy who'd tried to gas himself in the garage but it didn't take or he tried to hang himself from a pipe with an extension cord and the pipe busted open and he had to call someone to fix it because he was useless with pipes. I ran after him. He was slow, a shambling mess, and I tackled him in the sand next to one of the metal orange garbage cans that lined the beach. "Don't do this, Vlad," I said. "Make it easy."

Vlad started crying. Big, horrible Russian tears. He blubbered against me. "I am just one of God's children," he said. "I have lived a life of mistakes. I have not pleased God. My wife, she is a saint. My son is a saint. All these saints around me, and I just keep making mistakes."

I pushed him away from me.

"Do you understand?" he said. His eyes, black and troubled, looked like distressed coins. "If you punish me, you're punishing my wife, my son." His hands were up in a gesture of repentance.

I turned to the water. "Forget it," I said to Vlad over my shoulder. "Go be with your son."

I went back to Rosalia's. I gave Mama Fanny the hundred bucks from Magnuson. I sat alone with Rosalia, who was sleeping again, and stroked her hair. Mama Fanny made coffee in the kitchen. I started to tell Rosalia a story for something to do. "We're back in high school," I said. "We're in your room. Your mom is outside, listening to the radio. Your dad is washing the car. We have the radio on. The door is locked, even though they keep telling us not to lock it. We're kissing on the bed. I keep pushing your teddy bears on the floor, and you keep picking them up. You tell me to be gentle with them. You're wearing that black sweater you used to wear all the time. I put my hands inside it. I feel the wiry part of your bra. Your skin is goose-pimply. I kiss your neck. It's the best feeling in the world, having my hands under your shirt. We go into the closet, still kissing. It's always better in the closet because there's another door between us and your parents. I pull your sweater off over your head."

Mama Fanny knocked and came into the room. She had a demitasse cup balanced on a saucer.

I was sorry to have to stop talking to Rosalia like that.

"This is just so kind of you, Foley," Mama Fanny said, handing me the coffee.

"I'm sorry I can't do more," I said.

"You do too much already."

We just sat there, and I sipped my coffee. "Mr. Campagna okay today?"

She put her hand up. "He doesn't want help. He doesn't want to pray with me."

"I'll have more money soon," I said. I stood up and touched Rosalia's hand and then I left the room, placing the cup in the sink on my way back through the kitchen.

Mama Fanny followed me. "God bless you," she said. "Oh, God bless you."

I didn't look back at her. I walked out the front door, and I didn't look at the statue either. The street was all I wanted to see. I finished the story I'd been telling Rosalia in my head. *I pull your sweater off. I kiss the black bows on your bra. I stick my thumb in your belly button as a joke, but you hate when I do that. I tickle your armpits. We put a hand down each other's pants at the same time and laugh. The pants make everything more difficult, but we don't take them off. We're working together like one thing. It's the world. It's the best thing we'll ever know.*

The next smoker was at a different place. A garage on Nostrand Avenue. The guy I was fighting looked like Glass Joe from the Tyson video game I played as a kid. And he fell like Glass Joe too, swiveling to the canvas like a wet mop.

After the fight, in the car, Magnuson slipped me another hundred. "It's not a fluke maybe," he said. "We'll get you a trainer maybe. You'd like that?"

"Sure," I said.

"I know a guy. Queasy Marie's brother-in-law. And he knows a good cutman. Few months we'll get you some amateur bouts. For now it's this underground shit all the way." He reached out and slapped my cheek. "Fucking *Raging Bull*."

"I don't know. These guys aren't much."

Jackie Kiddo, who was driving, chimed in: "Kid, you've got power. I've seen the real deal. You're not in shape for it yet, but you can be sculpted."

I leaned back and closed my eyes.

"About Vlad," Magnuson said. "I never saw that dough."

"He had a kid with him," I said.

"I give a fuck for a kid?" Magnuson took out a gun and held it across his lap. "Now, I ain't gonna ruin you, but I can't just let it pass."

Jackie Kiddo pulled over. We were on a dark stretch of Stillwell under the El. Parked across from a liquor store with its riot gates down.

"Get out of the car," Magnuson said.

I didn't feel nervous. It was cold out, and I was in my cut-off sweats. I got out and felt the weather in my bones. I shivered. "I'll get what Vlad owes," I said.

"Kneel."

Jackie Kiddo was still behind the wheel. I looked over at him. He had a racing form open in his lap.

I got to my knees. Magnuson said, "You're fighting tomorrow night. At Jackie's." He held the gun over my shoulder and fired close to my ear. The bullet rocketed into the deep stretch of sidewalk behind us. The world went soundless. Gold threaded my vision. I heard God's voice in the loudness of the silence and it sounded like something that radios do when they're fuzzed up on a dead channel.

The next day Mama Fanny found me strange in my silence. The world still rang from the edges in. I could hear again but everything seemed to be coming at me from a distance. It was like being inside a bell. I gave Mama Fanny the money and went into Rosalia's room. I sat on the corner of her bed. *Dear Rosalia: I am sitting beside you now. I am telling you the story of the beginning of this new thing. I hope you can hear me. I hope you're still my girlfriend. Or I hope you're my girlfriend again. We both live in bells. I know what I need to do for us.*

I expected to hear Rosalia's voice somehow, but it didn't come.

It was Magnuson who did this to you. I don't know how, but he rattled you from the inside. Made you stroke out.

Rosalia's eyes opened. Her swallows got heavier. Her eyelids were raw and crusty. I saw pain pulsing in her face.

Mama Fanny, as if she had sensed Rosalia waking up, came into the room. "There's my girl," she said. "I'm so glad you're finally awake for Foley. You remember Foley, sweetie?"

I touched Rosalia's hand.

Mama Fanny had a plastic cup of applesauce in her hand, and she fed some to Rosalia with a demitasse spoon. The applesauce dribbled down Rosalia's chin. "Foley's taken a vow of silence today," Mama Fanny said.

I could talk, but I didn't want to. Words tasted like bricks in my mouth. I wanted to communicate with Rosalia some other way. And I had. The way her eyes opened, I knew something had crossed between us.

Rosalia gurgled applesauce in the back of her throat.

We talked through our eyes. She told me the story of all her quiet sadnesses. I told her that I'd been a chump but I was done being a chump. We kissed on the bridge of our gazes.

* * *

Communicating like that had taken something out of Rosalia, and she needed to rest. I went back to Uncle Harry's and we turned over milk crates in the alley and passed a fifth of schnapps back and forth. "You're fucked, boy," Uncle Harry said. His voice sounded tiny. "I can see it in your eyes."

I didn't say anything. Just slugged.

"Magnuson's got your voice?" Uncle Harry said.

"I'm okay," I said, and it was the first time I'd heard my own voice since Magnuson fired the gun over my shoulder. It came from deep inside the bell and sounded hollow.

"What'd he do to you, boy?"

I opened up to Uncle Harry and told him all of it. I must have sounded crazy when I said what I said about hearing God and communicating with Rosalia, but he didn't blink. He was my uncle and he was there to pass the schnapps to me. He just nodded and fingered his gums the whole time. When I was done, he said, "I got something for you." He went inside and came out with a machete in a nylon carrying case.

"What am I gonna do with that?" I said.

"Cut your way through everything, kid."

IV.

I walked and dreamed at the same time. In my dreams, I cut through tangles of glass. I cut through saints' beards. I cut through tall fires on Neptune. I cut through vines of smoke curling up under the El like sleeping snakes. I cut through the ghosts of The Terminal. I saw my father and I cut him down. I cut through the dark. I cut through flowers on the sidewalk. I cut through the Elephant Hotel and Luna Park and the shapes that the past made on Coney. Texas was a speck in front of me and I sliced it into quarters. My mother in Guatemala floated in the air and I cut her until she shattered. I cut the yellow out of the street. I cut the rain from the gutters. I cut through all the garbage. I cut through the screaming seagulls. I cut, I cut, I cut.

When I arrived at Jackie Kiddo's, I saw that the garage was cleared of cars. Tires were piled against the wall. A ring had been set up over one of the lifts. Folding chairs circled it. A framed picture of the Sacred Heart of Jesus was centered on the wall behind the ring; it might have always been there, I'd never noticed, but the ring had been hoisted up under it so Christ could watch.

The garage was smoky. I saw Jackie Kiddo through glass, back in his office. He was on the phone, pinching his nose with one hand, shuffling through a pile of receipts with the other. He didn't see me.

I walked around the ring. The garage, quartered through the ropes, with its Sacred Heart of Jesus and churchy smokiness, looked like the basement of Our Lady of Solace, where I'd done a lock-in as a kid. We spent all night there, drinking coffee and eating cookies and talking about Jesus, me and about fifteen other kids and a priest and a couple of nuns. I was twelve. It was the first time I'd stayed up all night. The priest, Father Riccardi, showed us *Rocky* and told us it was a religious movie. Then we listened to "All You Need is Love" by The Beatles on repeat and Father Riccardi danced around and acted the way I'd never seen a priest act. I didn't know Rosalia yet. I had a crush on Helen Pena. Now I tasted cookies crumbling in my mouth and thought of sweet Helen, who swayed her head to The Beatles, who put her hands over her eyes during the fight scenes in *Rocky*. I thought of her blue tights and the beaded cross she wore on fishing line around her neck.

Jackie spotted me from the office and put his hand up, like *Wait a sec, I'll be right there.*

I got into the ring and went down to my knees and took the shape of a praying man. I put the machete in front of me and took it out of its case. It didn't catch any light. It looked like a dark slit in the canvas.

Jackie came over and said, "Fucking holy man over here."

I did feel holy.

"This Chinese kid is who you're fighting tonight. His father's a dick. I hope you knock the fucker's head off."

I answered with closed eyes.

Jackie said, "Don't take last night personal. That's just a lesson is all. Magnuson likes you. Don't fuck with him again and you'll be a goddamn star."

Jackie had somehow helped Magnuson destroy Rosalia. As he climbed into the ring, I picked up the machete and Jackie saw it cross in front of me. His eyes went panicky. I saw him the way I'd seen everything in my walking dream, as a thing to cut through, just like Uncle Harry said.

And I did cut. I cut good. I opened Jackie up there in the ring. He sang in whimpers, said his *pleases* and *don'ts*. But I was quiet in my work. His guts spilled like blistered ribbons and painted the ring in dark swishes.

I crossed myself, the way my mother taught me to do when I was passing a Catholic church, any Catholic church. Then I left the ring and climbed, bloody, to the roof. The pigeons were in their coop. Magnuson was nowhere to be seen. The night sizzled with noises: horns, tire squeals, wheezing buses, alarms, sirens, shouts. I put the machete down. I opened the pigeon coop and told the pigeons to go. They took off in formation and circled overhead. I stopped one from leaving. The last one. White-splattered gray. I held him in my hands like I was a gentle saint, keeping his wings in place. The pigeon cooed. I stroked his small head. I sat on the ledge of the roof and waited for Magnuson. The other pigeons flew straight away from us and I watched them as long as I could, until the dark ate them up.

Cars arrived below. Men with cigars got out and hugged, kissed cheeks, cursed. Soon the Caddies and Escalades were double and triple-parked. The crowd entered the garage. No one saw me on the roof. I spotted the Chinese fighter. He had a military haircut and tattoos and a puffy face. Magnuson was the last to show, Peggy Sorensen on his arm. Magnuson, who had infected Rosalia with doom. Magnuson, who would make a cripple of me, too. Magnuson, whose pigeons were prisoners.

I tried to imagine inside the garage, what all the men were saying about Jackie Kiddo gutted in the ring.

I knew they'd be leaving soon. No one would want to be in the same place as the body.

The mass exit was calm, organized. The cars, like the pigeons, spread out in formation and then flitted away under the streetlights.

Magnuson showed on the roof, as I knew he would. The moon glowed behind him. He saw blood on me. He had that gun, the one he'd shot off over my shoulder. "Poor Jackie," he said.

I stroked the pigeon.

"You fucking let my pigeons go?" he said. He looked up at the night sky like someone who was seeing it for the first time. He was hoping his pigeons would cut a hole in the dark, return to him, land on his shoulders and head, let him wave his black flag.

"What you did to Rosalia, you're gonna pay," I said.

"Your mind's fucked, kid."

I let the last pigeon go. I wanted Magnuson to see how easy it was to stop being a prisoner, for him to know that his pigeons didn't love him.

The pigeon swooped down to the street and landed on the rim of a wire garbage can. Magnuson went to the edge of the roof and looked at the pigeon. He didn't say anything. He turned to me with the gun.

I didn't want to use the machete. I left it on the ground. I wasn't afraid of that gun. I wasn't afraid of Magnuson. I knew he'd whispered demon-like into Rosalia and shaken her from the soul up. I told him he couldn't take sound from me. I told him he couldn't take love. I told him I'd battle evil like him.

He said, "Kid, I'll have everyone you love killed. I'll start with the vegetable. Then it'll be Uncle Harry. I'll send my guy to Austin, to Guatemala. You're fucked in the head. There's an easy remedy."

I howled like a god who'd stolen the voice of a wolf.

The gun steadied in Magnuson's palm. He was frozen enough not to fire.

I saw myself from outside of myself. My fist seemed to leap from my hip. I hit Magnuson under the chin with an uppercut and he stumbled back two steps, losing his balance and dropping the gun. I hit him again and he went over the edge and landed about ten feet away from his pigeon, who remained perched on the rim of the garbage can. I didn't see blood coming from Magnuson. I saw only his body twisted in unnatural ways. I thought of the first time I'd seen him, naked in the hallway at Uncle Harry's, and now he was naked in the way that only the dead get naked. It felt good to see him like that, to know that he would never shake Rosalia from the inside again.

Down in Magnuson's office, I found a thick stack of hundreds in a manila envelope on his desk. I found more cash in a shoebox on the floor, ten grand maybe. It was all for Rosalia.

The old Dodge beater Magnuson had let me use to collect was parked back behind the garage. I started it. The car felt damp from some mysterious blessing. I drummed the wheel. I sang "All You Need is Love."

I drove to Bay Thirty-Eighth and parked at a hydrant across from Rosalia's. I rang the bell, which seemed to swell like a church organ in the night. Mama Fanny opened the door, and I must have been marked by the things I'd done because she greeted me like a savior. She fell to her knees and wept. I fed money to the pockets of her awful housedress. Hundreds exploded from her. "Oh, Foley," she said.

I touched her head. My wolf voice was gone. "I talked to Rosalia," I said.

Mama Fanny wept harder. I swear she wept oil. She shed hundreds like dying leaves.

"It's okay," I said.

I went to Rosalia and picked her up. She was as light as a bouquet of flowers. Her voice thrummed in her throat. Her eyes rocketed around. I put her over my shoulder. Her warmth tightened around me.

I carried her to the kitchen, where Mama Fanny moved on her knees. Mr. Campagna was standing next to her, wearing a stained wife-beater, his bare arms leathery. He was holding a jug of homemade wine across his belly. He wasn't crying. His cheeks and chin looked like they'd been thumbed by fire. I walked past them and out of the house.

I put Rosalia in the backseat of the car and drove her to the beach. I carried her to the shoreline. I sat in the sand and held her. Her body was alive. I wrote love notes to her in my head; I told her I'd fight for her forever. I know she received them. Her eyes told me yes. I prayed and prayed and prayed. *Let us be bones* was my prayer.

ABOUT THE AUTHOR:

William Boyle is the author of the novel *Gravesend*.

ACKNOWLEDGMENTS

Earlier versions of some of these stories appeared in the following magazines: "Death Don't Have No Mercy," *Thuglit*; "Yank Byrd's Idea for a Book, Late Summer 1992," *Out of the Gutter*; "Poor Box," *Chiron Review* and *Hardluck Stories*; "Zero at the Bone," *Battling Boxing Stories*; "Far from God," *Plots With Guns*; "Poughkeepsie," *Needle: A Magazine of Noir*; and "In the Neighborhood," *Lazy Fascist Review*. Thanks to the editors of these magazines, especially Anthony Neil Smith, Steve Weddle, and Cameron Pierce.

I wrote four of these stories—"Death Don't Have No Mercy," "Poor Box," "Zero at the Bone," and "Far from God"—when my wife and I were living in the Throggs Neck section of The Bronx (where her family is from and where her dad owned a bar for a long time). Thanks to Uncle Bobby Farrell, Betsy and Ed, and all the great bars on Tremont.

The other stories I wrote in Oxford, Mississippi. Both "Yank Byrd's Idea for a Book, Late Summer 1992" and "Poughkeepsie" were written for a class I took with Barry Hannah. I came to Oxford to study with Barry, and I'll always be grateful I got to take that one class with him before he passed away. He liked "Yank Byrd" and that meant a lot to me. "Poughkeepsie" started as a story called "Burn It Clean"—it was a flop at first and it took me about five years to get right. Thanks to Barry and thanks also to Larry Brown, one of my writing heroes, gone four years by the time I made it to Oxford, probably the main reason why I'm here.

I wrote "In the Neighborhood" over a couple of weeks when my wife, son, and I were between apartments, and Tom Franklin and Beth Ann Fennelly were nice enough to let us stay at their place while they were in Europe. It was summer, almost 100 degrees for two weeks straight. Wimbledon was on TV. My son was sick. I woke up at six every morning and went out to Tom's studio and hoped for a little of his good magic. I wound up writing one of the saddest and most fucked up things I've ever written. I can't thank Tom and Beth Ann enough for their support and friendship over the past few years.

"Here Come the Bells" is the newest story here. I thought it was going to be a novel and then it wasn't. I wrote it for a Broken River Books boxing anthology that David was planning. Thanks to David for everything.

Thank you: Matthew Revert; Alex Shakespeare; Jimmy Cajoleas; Jack Pendarvis; Ace Atkins; Megan Abbott; Willy Vlautin; Richard Lange; Scott Phillips; Chris Offutt; Anya Groner; Burke Nixon; Abby Greenbaum; John Hodges; Elizabeth Kaiser; John & Heather Brandon; Dave Newman & Lori Jakiela; Lee Durkee; Bobby Rea; David Swider; Scott Barretta; Casey Mitchem; Jed Ayres; Rachel Smith & Kevin Fitchett; Ryan Bubalo; Josh Murray; Anthony Moretta; Tyler Keith; Gary Short; Phil McCausland; Andy Paul; McKay McFadden; James Barry; Square Books, especially Cody Morrison & Lisa Howorth; Oxford Public Library, especially LB Walker; Thacker

Mountain Radio; Proud Larry's for Noir at the Bar; Good Idea Club; all my other Oxford pals; my family & friends in Brooklyn & New Paltz.

Thank you to the Farrell Clan—too many generous and kind people to name.

Thank you to my mother & my grandmother for their unending support and love. My grandfather passed away this past year, and I've never missed someone so goddamn much. My Uncle Joe also passed away. Both deaths hit me hard. I'm so sorry they're gone. I wish they were still here.

As always, everything is for Katie, Eamon, & Connolly Jean.

Printed in Great Britain
by Amazon